"You still have a spot of mascara under your eye."

"I do?" He studied his reflection in the rearview mirror. "Yeah, so I do."

Cheyenne rummaged in her purse. "Let me clean that off." She pulled out a tissue.

Derek threw his arm across the back of the bench seat and leaned toward her.

She dabbed the tissue under his eye, feeling his gaze on her. Their faces were so close—a little tingle went up her spine at his nearness. She wiped the tissue under his lashes one last time, wishing she could stay a few more minutes, but her job was done. "There, that's better." She looked into his eyes.

His gaze held hers. "Much better." His eyes dipped down to her lips.

Cheyenne caught a quick breath. He was going to kiss her!

But Derek suddenly cleared his throat and sat back. "Thanks." Placing a fist against his mouth, he coughed. "Uh, guess I'll see you Sunday at church."

DONNA REIMEL ROBINSON is a member of JOY Writers, a local critique group. As a pastor's wife, she plays the piano for their church. In her spare time, Donna enjoys sewing and reading. The Robinsons have four children, two children-in-law, and six grandchildren. They live in Denver, Colorado. Visit Donna's website at www.donnarobinsonbooks.com.

Books by Donna Reimel Robinson

HEARTSONG PRESENTS
HP838—For the Love of Books
HP926—The Thing About Beauty

No One But You

Donna Reimel Robinson

Heartsong Presents

This book is dedicated to my Savior, Jesus Christ, who called me to write according to His own purpose, and also to my daughter, Holly Marie Robinson Armstrong, who is a great "first editor." Thanks for all your help, Holly!

A note from the Author:
I love to hear from my readers! You may correspond with me by writing:

Donna Reimel Robinson
Author Relations
PO Box 721
Uhrichsville, OH 44683

ISBN 978-1-61626-336-2

NO ONE BUT YOU

All scripture quotations are taken from the King James Version of the Bible.

All of the characters and events in this book are fictitious. Any resemblance to actual persons, living or dead, or to actual events is purely coincidental.

Our mission is to publish and distribute inspirational products offering exceptional value and biblical encouragement to the masses.

PRINTED IN THE U.S.A.

one

Cheyenne Wilkins perched on the edge of the red leather chair in the law office of Mr. Barton Griggs, her heart beating an erratic tempo as she listened to the lawyer read her grandmother's will. Since Grandmother Ingersoll's death seven months ago, she had been hoping she would inherit some money, but she didn't expect this.

Mr. Griggs laid his reading glasses on the mahogany desk. "So that's it." He raised bushy white eyebrows as his gray eyes glanced from Cheyenne to her dad, Jim Wilkins.

She lifted her hands, palms up. "I have to be married? And have a child?" She exchanged a glance with her dad. He looked just as stunned as she felt.

The lawyer nodded. "I tried to talk your grandmother into putting the money in a trust fund for you, but she had her own stubborn ideas." Mr. Griggs gave her a sad smile. "She wrote this will shortly after your grandfather died and long after your mother had died. You were a teenager, Cheyenne."

Dad gave a grudging nod. "I'm sure she thought you'd be married and have two or three kids by the age of thirty."

"Yes." Mr. Griggs steepled his fingers. "And even though Florence turned eccentric toward the end, she was in her right mind when she made the will. I can't find any loopholes to change it."

Cheyenne's shoulders drooped. "I'll never inherit that money. My birthday is next week, and I'll be twenty-eight."

The lawyer leaned back in his chair. "You have two years, Cheyenne. Surely you'll find someone to marry before then."

"What happens to the money if Cheyenne doesn't meet the conditions of the will?" Dad folded his arms.

Mr. Griggs straightened the papers on his desk. "All the

recipients in Florence Ingersoll's will are dead, except for Cheyenne and George Sommers."

Cheyenne willed her pulse to slow down. "Who is this George Sommers?"

Dad's blue eyes met hers. "A distant relative of your grandfather's. I believe he was in the restaurant business." He waved a beefy hand toward the lawyer. "Florence must have liked him to include him in the will. Either she really liked someone and couldn't do enough for them, or she didn't like them at all." He grimaced.

Lowering her eyes, Cheyenne felt a stab of pain for her dad. Bitterness laced his words, and her mind went back to a conversation she once had with her grandmother. Cheyenne had only been seventeen, but she remembered every word.

Jim Wilkins was not good enough to marry my daughter, and he's still not good enough." Grandmother's blue eyes flashed, and her white hair quivered as she ranted. *"If it hadn't been for your grandfather intervening, Lynn would have married William Thorndyke. He would have taken care of her."*

Cheyenne still recalled the shock she felt. Grandmother had always been kind to her, maybe because she was her only grandchild, but evidently her kindness didn't extend to Jim Wilkins.

Mr. Griggs donned his glasses. "Sommers is the only other relative of Mrs. Ingersoll's who is still living." He shuffled some papers. "Ah! Here's the information. The man lives in Reno, Nevada, and has expanded his restaurant to include a hotel and a casino."

"A casino?" Dad frowned as he glanced at Cheyenne. "So if my daughter doesn't fulfill the requirements of her grandmother's will, Sommers will get the four million dollars?"

Mr. Griggs nodded. "That is correct."

"Without any stipulations on his part?"

"None whatsoever."

I can't believe this! Cheyenne sighed. "So if I'm not married in two years, with a child, all of Grandmother's money will go to this casino owner?"

Mr. Griggs shrugged. "I'm sorry, Cheyenne."

"Don't give up yet." Dad's eyes met hers. "A lot can happen in two years."

She looked down. *But will it?*

two

On Saturday, June 20th, Cheyenne stood in the church lobby, waiting her turn to walk down the center aisle of the auditorium. *Always a bridesmaid, never a bride.* But she hoped to be a bride soon, and in this very church in Fort Lob, Wyoming.

If only she had a groom.

The white carnations in her bouquet shook slightly, and she took a deep breath before smoothing down the sky-blue satin of her long bridesmaid gown. She glanced around at the other bridesmaids dressed in different shades of pink, yellow, green, and violet. Cheyenne was thankful she had been given a blue dress since it brought out the blue in her eyes.

"I can't believe my little sister's getting married," Callie Hutchins whispered. She was wearing a light-green dress, which didn't do a thing for her dark eyes.

Cheyenne smiled at her best friend. "I love weddings, and this one's going to be so pretty." She glanced at the front of the auditorium. The men stood on the platform, waiting for the ten attendants in Tonya Brandt's wedding. There were only four men, two standing on each side of the groom. Four women would join them on the platform, and the other six girls would stand below, forming a circle of pastel "flowers"—as Tonya described it.

Callie leaned toward her. "By the way, happy birthday."

"Thanks!" That was all Cheyenne had thought of today. A pang of apprehension stabbed her. She had exactly two years to fulfill the conditions of Grandmother's will, which was never far from her mind.

No use thinking about that during Tonya's wedding, although she wished she could tell Callie about the will. But

Mr. Griggs was adamant that she and Dad keep that info to themselves.

She turned to Callie with a smile. "Dad already gave me a present this morning at breakfast."

Callie raised her eyebrows. "What was it?"

"A ruby necklace he had given Mom when they were dating. I never saw it before, and I love it!"

"That was thoughtful of him. It's something you can remember your mom by."

"Yeah, I'm planning to wear it to church tomorrow."

Evelyn Seymour, the wedding coordinator, hushed them as she walked by. She adjusted her black-rimmed glasses. "Be ready for your turn, girls." She waved her sheaf of papers toward the auditorium.

Cheyenne glanced behind her at the bride. Tonya stood beside her father, Jake Brandt, with her arm laced through his. She looked beautiful, as always, with her perfect complexion and dark hair and eyes. A tiny tiara crowned her head, and a veil flowed down her back. Jake stood tall and confident, as well he should be. He'd already given away three daughters—Melissa, Callie, and Molly. He must be a pro at this by now.

With a last glance at Tonya, Cheyenne held in a sigh. The tiny sequins sewn on the lace of Tonya's bridal gown, which she had designed herself, glinted in the overhead lights as she moved. But it was the bride's figure that Cheyenne envied. The dress had a fitted waist, and Tonya's waist must have a smaller diameter than one of Cheyenne's thighs.

I haven't been that thin since I was ten!

The organ music changed, and Evelyn waved her papers. "That's your cue, girls." She corralled the first six girls to the door, and they walked down the aisle, two by two, and then fanned out across the front of the auditorium as they rehearsed last evening.

Cheyenne moved into place and stepped into the aisle at Evelyn's prompting. Sucking in her stomach, she smiled and slowly walked down the aisle, feeling curious eyes on her from every crowded pew as she moved past.

As she neared the platform, she glanced ahead at the groom. Murray Twichell smiled back at her as he stood beside Pastor Reilly. Her glance flitted to Jon Hunt, the best man, and then landed on Derek Brandt. He was her destination.

Pinching the satin skirt of her gown, she pulled up the fabric a couple of inches and ascended the three steps of the platform. She raised her eyes to Derek's handsome face as she drew nearer. He smiled at her, his dark-blue eyes holding hers.

If only that look and smile meant something! But it had been rehearsed last night, as per Evelyn's instructions. With an inward sigh, Cheyenne turned to face the audience, standing as close to Derek as she dared.

Melissa walked the length of the aisle and ascended the platform on the other side, sharing a smile with her husband, Philip, before stopping at his side. Then it was Molly's turn. After walking up the stairs, she stood beside Jon, near Cheyenne. Callie came down the aisle last, as the matron of honor. Her husband, Lane, smiled at her as she took her place between him and the pastor.

The music changed once again, and the congregation stood to turn and watch the bride. Tonya seemed to float down the aisle on her father's arm. A beautiful smile lit her face as she gazed at her groom.

Tears crept to Cheyenne's eyes, and she sent up a silent prayer. *Oh Lord, this is what I want.* She had been in love with Derek since high school, ever since he asked her to the prom when he was a junior and she was a senior. But for the past ten years, their relationship had deadlocked into being nothing more than good pals. He seemed to enjoy spending time with her, but they always hung out in a group. Would he ever view her as more than a friend?

And now with Grandmother's will hanging over her head...

She glanced across the platform as Tonya and Jake stopped

in front of the pastor. All the couples in the bridal party were married to each other—except for her and Derek. Melissa and Philip, Callie and Lane, Molly and Jon, and now, of course, Tonya and Murray. They were all part of the Brandt family, too.

Is that a sign, Lord?

Derek didn't plan to get married until he was forty. At least, that's what he told his sisters. Evidently he enjoyed living at home, letting his mom make his meals and do his laundry, and working on that huge sheep ranch with his dad.

But Cheyenne wasn't about to let him remain single, not with the Last Will and Testament of Florence Ingersoll pressing her into marriage. As the ceremony progressed, her determination increased at the same time. She would lose weight and make a concentrated effort to win Derek's hand.

Win *his* hand? That would be a role reversal, but she couldn't depend on Mr. Laid-Back to win *her* hand. If she left it up to Derek, she would be forty-one years old before they married, if they married at all.

And that would definitely invalidate Grandmother's will.

Tonya and Murray repeated their vows, gazing into each other's eyes. Cheyenne could only see Tonya's face, but she envied the look of love the bride held for her bridegroom. A wistful sigh escaped Cheyenne's lips. Maybe someday. . .but not too far into the future.

Next week would be good.

ða

Derek relaxed on the blue chair in the living room, thankful the wedding was over and he was now wearing comfortable clothes. Why did people have to make such a big fuss about weddings anyway?

After the cake-only reception at the church, all the Brandt relatives had descended on the house en masse, and the noise level drifted up to the ceiling and bounced back to Derek. He laid his head back on the chair and watched the ceiling fan turn in lazy circles. His eyes began to close when a commotion roused him.

"Hey, everybody." Tonya, dressed now in a classy skirt and blouse, stood in the middle of the living room, her dark eyes shining. "Before Murray and I leave, we all have to sing 'Happy Birthday' to Cheyenne." She nodded to her husband. "Ready?"

Murray started the song, and everyone joined in.

Easing out of his chair, Derek rumbled in on the third line. He glanced at Cheyenne, standing near the fireplace. Her round face sported a smile, and Derek thought the two deep dimples in her cheeks made her cute.

When the song ended, she nodded at the crowd. "Thanks, everyone! I've had a wonderful birthday."

Derek kept his eyes on Cheyenne as she hugged a few well-wishers, and something stirred deep inside him. He and Cheyenne had been best buddies for years, but sometimes it hit him how pretty she was.

"Okay, folks." Dad strode through the living room. "Time for the happy couple to leave. I'll get my car keys."

Tonya and Murray followed him but stopped every few seconds to receive hugs from the many aunts, uncles, and cousins, not to mention brothers and sisters, who lined the room.

Derek waited until Murray stepped in front of him. "Is Dad driving you guys to Denver?"

"Yep." Murray looked up at him. "We're staying at The Brown Palace Hotel tonight. Our flight leaves Denver International Airport at one o'clock tomorrow afternoon."

"Stay safe, Twitch." Derek shook Murray's hand. "I hope you two have a great honeymoon in Hawaii."

"We will." Murray cocked an eyebrow at him before he smiled.

Derek grinned. Twitch got the girl he wanted.

"Bye, Derek!" Tonya threw her arms around his shoulders.

He hugged her. "Have fun, sis. We'll be praying for a safe trip."

"Thanks."

The crowd followed the happy couple to the door and flowed outside behind them. Everyone waved as they drove off, with Mom and Grandma waving handkerchiefs, and then they all tramped back into the house.

Above the din of the noisy relatives, Lane tapped Derek on the shoulder. "Callie wants to eat at Mama's Kitchen in Lusk for a nice quiet dinner. Want to go with us? I'm paying."

"Sure. I'm always game for a free meal at a good restaurant."

Lane grinned. "I'll let her know. Most of the relatives are leaving, and Mom is going to Casper with Grandma for a week. Callie wants to say good-bye to everyone. Then the four of us will go out to eat."

Derek frowned. "The four of us?"

"Callie invited Cheyenne."

"Oh." Derek watched Lane wend his way past several uncles out to the kitchen. Was this date Callie's idea? His sisters were always trying to throw Cheyenne and him together.

Not that there was anything wrong with Cheyenne. He glanced around the crowded living room, but she was gone. If he ever got married, Cheyenne Wilkins would be the kind of wife he would choose—godly, vivacious, pretty.

But for the past several years, Derek felt the Lord wanted him to stay single in order to serve Him. And the Lord was keeping him busy. Besides his regular volunteer work at the orphanage in Casper, he planned to help build a church in Honduras in October. Then there was the soup kitchen that requested volunteers during the holidays.

The last thing Derek needed was a dating relationship. He knew that dating a girl took time and money. But it wouldn't hurt to go out on this impromptu date with Cheyenne.

Besides, it was her birthday.

❧

"Don't tell the waiter it's my birthday." Cheyenne whispered the words to Callie, using her tall menu to not only guide her words across the table, but to keep Derek and Lane from hearing. "All the servers will sing to me."

"But they'll give you a free cake." Callie spoke so softly that Cheyenne had to read her lips.

Cheyenne lowered her own voice to almost nonexistent. "That's the problem. I'm trying to lose weight."

"You don't have to eat it." Callie motioned sideways with her head. "Give it to Derek."

"But if it gets too close to me, I won't be able to help myself."

Derek cleared his throat. "What are you girls whispering about?"

"Nothing." Cheyenne laid her menu on the table as she glanced at Derek sitting beside her. "I think I'll order the soup and salad." She took a sip of her water.

He looked back at his menu. "I'm getting the lasagna."

"Sounds good to me." Across the table, Lane closed his menu and looked at his wife. "What about you, Callie?"

She was hidden behind her menu. "I'm still deciding."

The waiter, a short man with a mop of black hair and a thick mustache, stopped at their table. "Are you ready to order this evening?" He had a charming Italian accent.

Derek motioned toward Cheyenne. "She'll have the soup and salad, and I'll take the lasagna."

"Very good." The waiter pulled a pad from his white apron pocket and wrote it down.

Cheyenne's heart swelled. Derek had ordered for her, like they were on a real date! She had been apprehensive about how he would react to this double date, but now she relaxed, leaning a little closer to him.

An hour later the waiter came to collect their dirty dishes. Cheyenne could have eaten more, but she wanted to leave hungry, hoping it would make her a pound or two lighter.

The waiter glanced around as he picked up the salad bowl. "Did you save room for dessert?"

Callie shook her head. "I'm too full."

"So am I," Cheyenne agreed, even though it wasn't quite true.

Like a common hitchhiker, Derek pointed his thumb

at Cheyenne as he addressed the waiter. "It's her birthday today."

Cheyenne gasped. "Derek! You would have to bring that up!"

He grinned at her.

The waiter inclined his head toward her. "It will be our pleasure to sing to such a beautiful woman."

What a flirt! Cheyenne smiled at him. "Thanks."

In a few minutes, seven people surrounded their table, all dressed in white aprons. Instead of singing the traditional birthday song, they sang some other ditty, accompanied by hand clapping and feet stomping. When they finished, the waiter set a tiny cake in front of her, complete with piped frosting and a red rose in the center.

"Thank you." She smiled at the servers as they offered their congratulations before leaving.

Derek threw his arm around her shoulder and squeezed. "We got you good, Cheyenne."

She smiled back at him, his face only inches away. If only they were a bona fide couple! But in another second his arm lifted, and she felt the loss.

The waiter stood at the end of their table. "Would you like anything else for dessert?" His dark-brown eyes glanced between Lane and Derek.

Lane frowned. "Don't you have some type of cream puffs on the menu?"

"Ah yes, the cannoli." The waiter wrote it down and turned to Derek.

He shrugged. "I'll have the same."

When the waiter left, Cheyenne forced her fingers to slide the cake in front of Derek. "You can have this, too. I'm"—*on a diet*—"too full to eat it."

"Thanks." Derek picked up his extra fork then looked at Lane. "Want a bite?"

"Nah." Lane eyed the cake. "It's only big enough for one person."

"A single serving." Derek raised his eyebrows. "Just like my

Sunday school class, the Single Servings. Too bad you two aren't in my class anymore. We miss you."

Callie looked at her husband with a sly smile. "I'd rather be married."

Lane waggled his eyebrows at her. "We're not single servings anymore, are we, Callie? We're double portions."

Derek laughed.

"I just realized. . ." Cheyenne looked at Derek. "Tonya and Murray won't be in the Single Servings anymore either. If your class members keep getting married, you soon won't have a singles class."

"I'll be there." He leaned toward her, a pleading expression in his dark-blue eyes. "Don't leave me, okay?"

Before she could reply, the waiter brought two plates of cannoli to the table.

Cheyenne glanced at Callie, who hid a smile behind her water glass. Cheyenne smiled back, a little thrill running through her.

Someday she and Derek would be double portions—and by the end of this year, if she had anything to say about it.

three

On Sunday morning, Cheyenne adjusted the waistband of her black skirt as she opened her bedroom door. Dad's collie ran down the short hallway of their one-floor home and jumped on her, his nails scratching against her favorite gray blouse with silver hearts. He barked out a greeting as his tail wagged.

"Marshal! Get down." Cheyenne brushed her hand across her skirt. "Oh great. Now I'll have dog hair on me when I go to church." Her fingers slid across something wet. "Yuck! Dog slobber is even worse."

The collie sat down and panted, his almond-shaped eyes gazing up at her.

Cheyenne's heart melted. "Okay, I forgive you—especially when you smile at me like that."

Marshal came from a litter of collies from The Rocking B Ranch. The Brandt family always used collies as their sheepdogs, and Jake and Yvette had given Marshal to Dad as a birthday gift three years ago. Patting the dog on his head, Cheyenne walked past him and entered the kitchen. Her dad sat at the table, reading the Sunday paper. She perused her father. Jim Wilkins was dressed for church in a dark-green shirt with the cuffs rolled back, exposing his meaty hands and thick wrists.

Why did I have to inherit a Wilkins body? All her dad's brothers and sisters had big bones. On the other hand, her mom, who had died from leukemia when Cheyenne was eight years old, had been of average height and weight.

Opening a cupboard, she pulled out a coffee mug. "Good morning, Dad."

Glancing up, his blue eyes met hers. He ran his hand over

his full head of gray hair. "Morning, baby girl." His booming voice echoed in the small kitchen. "Sleep good?"

"I guess so." Cheyenne poured herself a cup of coffee. Dad had called her "baby girl" ever since she could remember.

Folding the paper, he laid it on the table and stood. A pink-flowered tie blossomed on his barrel-like chest. What decade had that tie come from? "Dad, why aren't you wearing the tie I picked out for you last night?"

Frowning, he lifted the end of the tie. "I like this one." He glanced at the clock on the stove. "I need to leave. I'm the greeter at church this morning."

She sighed. "Okay, Dad. I'll see you when I get there."

He pulled her into a quick bear hug before grabbing his keys. "See ya."

Dad was tall—six foot five. At least Cheyenne hadn't grown to *that* height. It was bad enough being almost six feet tall. And she was thankful she hadn't inherited his loud voice.

As she sipped her coffee, she glanced out the kitchen window. Dad backed his Town Car out the short driveway and roared off down the street toward church. Cheyenne fingered the ruby necklace Dad had given her yesterday— the necklace that had belonged to her mom. A melancholy feeling swept over her. She missed her mom. Dad had been a widower now for twenty years.

In the quiet, she heard her cell phone ring. Taking a quick walk back to her bedroom, she pulled the phone from her purse and glanced at the number. Marshal padded to her side as she flipped it open. "Hi, Callie!"

"Cheyenne, I need your help." She sounded agitated.

"What's up, girlfriend?"

"Lane is really sick this morning."

Cheyenne raised her eyebrows. "He was okay last night at the restaurant."

"That's the problem. I talked to my dad this morning, and Derek is sick, too. It was those cannoli. They must have been spoiled."

"Oh no." Cheyenne sank down to her bed, and Marshal laid his head in her lap. She stroked his tan fur. "What can I do to help?"

"Lane could use some ginger ale, but your dad's store is closed today. Could you possibly go over and get me a can? I'll pay him tomorrow."

"Don't worry about paying. I'll get a two-liter bottle for you." Cheyenne stood and grabbed her purse. "In fact, I'll give one to your dad for Derek."

"That would be great. Thanks, Chey."

They said their good-byes, and Cheyenne locked up the house, leaving Marshal inside. She walked back to the detached one-car garage. Dad let her park in the garage since her car, an olive-green Dodge Dart, needed to be babied. It broke down at least once every six months, but she'd bought it secondhand in high school and couldn't imagine getting rid of her classic antique.

After picking up two bottles of ginger ale at Wilkins Grocery and dropping off one at Callie's house, Cheyenne drove to the Brandt home and knocked on the back door.

Jake opened it. "Hi, Cheyenne." He adjusted his wire-rimmed glasses as he stepped back. "Come on in."

"Thanks." With a smile, she followed him through the mudroom. He was tall but not big like her dad, and he looked dignified in his Sunday suit.

Cheyenne stepped into the kitchen. "I got a call from Callie this morning. She said Lane and Derek are both sick." She held up the bottle of ginger ale. "I thought this might help Derek."

"Callie called me, too." Jake lifted a large black Bible from the kitchen table. "Derek wants me to teach his Sunday school class. Since Yvette's in Casper this week, I'm glad you came by." He took a set of keys from his pocket. "Would you mind staying? I really don't want to leave Derek alone all morning."

Cheyenne's lips parted before a thrill buzzed through

her. "Sure! I'd love to stay and help Derek out if he needs anything."

"That's great!" Jake motioned toward the living room. "He's out there on the sofa. Don't know if he'll want any ginger ale, but you can ask." He walked to the door. "I appreciate it, Cheyenne. See you later." He entered the mudroom, closing the door firmly behind him.

She grinned, reveling in the turn of events. *Thank You, Lord!* Maybe God let Derek get sick so they could spend another day together. Perhaps she could meet the conditions of Grandmother's will sooner than she thought.

Opening the ginger ale bottle, she poured some into a glass and added ice from the freezer. Then she walked through the dining room and into the living room. Derek lay on the sofa, dressed in sweatpants and a blue T-shirt. Dark circles rested under his closed eyes, and his face looked pale—except for the dark stubble on his jaw.

"Derek?"

His eyes opened and focused on her face. Her heart fluttered.

"Oh, Cheyenne," he murmured. "Why are you over here?"

"Callie told me you were sick." She held up the glass. "I brought you some ginger ale."

He moaned. "No thanks." Closing his eyes, he tightened his arms around his stomach. "I'll be okay."

Cheyenne set the glass on the end table. "Your dad asked me to stay with you this morning. I hope you don't mind." She held her breath, hoping he wouldn't tell her to leave.

"Yeah, whatever." He shivered.

"Are you cold?" Leaning over him, she placed her palm on his forehead. His skin wasn't burning, but it was warm. "You might have a fever. I'll get you a blanket."

She ran upstairs to the second floor, knowing she'd find extra bedding stashed in the hall linen closet. Pulling out a soft yellow blanket, she headed back downstairs. She covered Derek with the blanket and tucked it around his shoulders.

"That's better," he murmured. "Thanks."

"Are you sure you don't want some ginger ale?"

He screwed up his face. "Won't be able to keep it down. I found out at breakfast this morning—must have thrown up the last three days' worth of food in ten minutes."

"Oh." His words made Cheyenne a bit queasy herself. "I'm sorry those cannoli were spoiled."

"Yeah. They tasted a little strange, so I only ate one." Derek closed his eyes. "Good thing."

"Why don't you rest, Derek? I'll be out in the kitchen if you need me."

"Okay, thanks." He closed his eyes, his dark eyelashes lowering on his pale cheeks.

Cheyenne gazed at his handsome face. The day's growth of beard made him look like a pirate. With a wistful sigh, she turned toward the kitchen.

❧

"Cheyenne?"

At Derek's voice, she jumped up from the kitchen table. She had spent the past hour looking through Yvette's cookbooks and had decided to test a soup recipe. Turning to the stove, she lowered the burner before walking into the living room. Derek still lay on the sofa, but the color had returned to his face. "Do you need something?"

"Since we're missing church today, I wondered if you could read some scripture to me."

"I'd love to, but I left my Bible in the car." She glanced around. "Where's yours, Derek?"

"Upstairs. Next to my bed."

Again she climbed the stairway to the second floor, puffing a little as she reached the top. *I'm going to get rid of these extra twenty pounds!*

She walked down the hallway, knowing exactly where Derek's room was. He used to share it with his older brother until Ryan got married and moved to Denver. Both single beds were neatly made with navy comforters. A brown leather Bible sat on the nightstand. She picked it up, then took a moment to breathe in his scent. This was Derek's domain—a masculine room with a braided gray rug on the polished wood floor and an oak dresser between the windows. She glanced outside, catching a glimpse of the backyard that ended at the white barn. Beyond that was nothing but open fields. In the distance, a flock of sheep dotted the hillside.

Walking downstairs, she mentally compared all the acreage the Brandt family owned with the small parcel of land her dad had in town. Hundreds of houses like theirs could fit on the Brandts' property. But if she inherited Grandmother's money, she would share it with Dad. He had always wanted to have a bigger house on a couple acres of land.

She pulled a dining room chair near the sofa, sat down, and opened the Bible. "What do you want me to read?"

Derek's eyes opened to slits. "Psalm 23. 'The Lord is my shepherd.' Isn't that what you read when someone is dying?"

Cheyenne raised her eyebrows. "You're not that bad, are you?"

He rewarded her with a lazy grin. "Just kidding."

With a smile, she shook her head. Leave it to Derek to tease her, even when he was sick. "So do you want me to read the twenty-third Psalm, or do you have something else in mind?"

"Read John chapter 10."

Cheyenne turned the thin pages to the New Testament. "This is a shepherd passage, too."

"Yeah, well, I'm a shepherd." He cracked another smile.

Cheyenne's heart swelled. She loved being with Derek, talking to him, getting teased by him. "You must be feeling better."

He nodded. "I feel a lot better than I did this morning."

"Good." Looking down, she began reading. When she finished, she and Derek discussed the chapter for a few minutes.

He motioned toward the Bible. "Read verse 10 again."

She found the place. " 'The thief cometh not, but for to

steal, and to kill, and to destroy: I am come that they might have life, and that they might have it more abundantly.'"

He gave her a weak smile. "Love that verse—my favorite in the whole book." He stared at the ceiling. "The abundant life. That's a great concept—what Jesus wants to give Christians in this life, but so many want to go their own way."

"That's true." Cheyenne chewed on her lower lip. *He's so godly, Lord!*

"The Bible says if we abide in Christ and keep God's commandments, He'll bless us. He'll give us exceeding abundantly above all we can ask or think." He grinned. "That was your Sunday-morning sermon, Miss Wilkins, and I'm sure it blessed your heart beyond measure."

She laughed. "It certainly did."

"Kind of basic, actually." Derek sat up and sniffed. "What's that wonderful smell?"

"I made you some soup. It's simmering on the stove right now." She raised her eyebrows. "Are you ready to eat? It might make you feel better."

ஃ

Derek's stomach felt empty. "That would be great, Cheyenne." Throwing the blanket aside, he stood and wobbled a moment. He rubbed his chin, hoping she wouldn't notice how weak he was. "I should make a pit stop in the bathroom first. I probably look like three-day pond scum."

She laughed. "No you don't. You look. . .good."

"Only good?" He grinned at her.

"Well. . .I was going to say 'handsome,' but you always look handsome."

He folded his arms. "Are you trying to flirt with me?"

"Maybe." Giving him a wink, she turned toward the kitchen.

Derek watched her go. For the first time, he noticed that she was dressed for church, and her black skirt swished as she walked away. He'd always liked hanging around with Cheyenne, and he loved to tease her, but he had to be careful.

There was a fine line between teasing and flirting, and she seemed to want to cross it. He couldn't do that. He had to remain single—single for the Lord's work. Wasn't that God's will for him?

When he emerged from the bathroom, the smell of the soup drew him into the kitchen. He took a seat at the table.

Cheyenne turned from the stove. "How do you feel—now that you're up?"

"Hungry." He smiled at her. "What's for lunch?"

"Chicken noodle soup." Picking up a large spoon, she stirred it around in a pan. "I found some carrots and celery in the fridge, a package of egg noodles, and some chicken in the freezer." She turned to him. "I hope your mom doesn't mind if I used the chicken. She might have been saving it for something."

"She won't care." Cheyenne was making homemade soup? For him? He would have just opened a can and heated it up. As Derek watched her ladle the soup into two bowls, it struck him that Cheyenne had a servant's heart. "Hey, um, thanks for coming over and taking care of me. I really appreciate it."

"It was your dad's idea, but I didn't mind helping out." Setting the bowls and two spoons on the table, she took a seat across from him. "I didn't have anything to do at church this morning besides warm the pew. Sometimes I work in the nursery, but I wasn't on the schedule today."

He cocked an eyebrow at her. "You ended up taking care of a big baby anyway."

She laughed, a musical sound he enjoyed hearing. "Oh Derek, you're not hard to care for at all." Folding her hands, she raised her eyebrows at him. "Would you ask the blessing?"

"Sure." He bowed his head. "Father in heaven, thank You for providing all our needs, especially for healing me. Thank You for this good soup Cheyenne made. Bless her for coming over to help me. In Jesus' name. Amen."

Cheyenne tucked a strand of blond hair behind her ear

as she took a napkin from the holder on the table. Derek watched her. He had always liked that little trait she had—tucking her hair behind her ear. He lifted a spoonful of soup to his lips. The warm liquid felt good as he swallowed. "Hmm, this is great."

"Glad you like it." She took a sip.

"I hate missing church." Derek stirred his soup then lifted the spoon for another bite. "It doesn't seem like Sunday morning if I'm not teaching Sunday school."

"I'm sure your dad's doing a fine job." Cheyenne glanced at her watch. "Of course Sunday school's been over for an hour or so."

"True." Derek swallowed another spoonful before he spoke. "I hope Dad didn't forget to announce our bowling activity in two weeks, although he must not have had many students. Tonya and Murray are out of the picture now."

Cheyenne smiled, creasing her dimples. "And you and I weren't there either."

He rubbed the stubble on his chin. "Makes me wonder what people thought. They might start a rumor that we ran away together." As soon as the words left his mouth, Derek frowned. *Why did I say that?* He didn't want to give her any ideas.

But it was too late.

Cheyenne laughed. "Yeah! Let's run away! We'll give the ladies in this town some fuel for their gossip."

Derek didn't share her smile. "I was just kidding." He took another bite.

"I'm sorry." Cheyenne's smile lingered as she stirred her soup. "I guess we shouldn't give people things to gossip about. That's just wrong."

Despite his concern about her flirting, Derek grinned. Some girls were hard to talk to, but not Cheyenne.

Being with her was like putting on a pair of comfortable old shoes.

four

Almost two weeks later, Cheyenne drove up Highway 270 on her way back from Lusk. She had just finished her Thursday class, and tomorrow evening would be the last one. For the past week and a half, she had attended a class on the art of applying makeup, something she had always wanted to learn. Tomorrow evening was her test—applying makeup to another person's face.

The engine of her Dodge gave a sudden cough, and the front end rattled and shook violently.

"Oh no!" Cheyenne let up on the gas. With a wheeze, the engine died. Her shoulders slumped as she pulled over, letting the car roll to the side of the road. Getting out, she lifted the hood. Steam poured from the engine, and she jumped back.

"Oh great!" She really should invest in a new car, but her Dart was a familiar old friend. Emphasis on *old*.

Leaning against the side of the car, she folded her arms. The sun had already set over the Laramie Mountains, and her cell phone was useless out here in the boonies. The highway stretched out on either side of her, deserted, not a vehicle in sight.

Maybe Murray Twichell would drive by in his patrol car. This road was part of his section for the Wyoming Highway Patrol, and he and Tonya were back from their honeymoon in Hawaii. In fact Cheyenne had asked Tonya to come to her class tomorrow night for the makeup demonstration. The new bride had agreed to be her model, and Cheyenne couldn't have asked for a prettier face.

She glanced up and down the road again. Nothing. She looked up to the darkening sky. "Lord, help!"

Maybe she should try to start the car. The steam was gone, so perhaps the engine would start up. She got in and turned the key.

The engine started then sputtered and died.

Cheyenne dropped her head on the steering wheel. Would she be here all night? *Lord, please send someone!*

A few minutes later, she heard the hum of a vehicle approaching. *Praise God!* She jumped out of the car and waved her arms at the two headlights, hoping it wasn't a serial killer.

A red pickup truck slowed down, pulled behind her car, and stopped.

The headlights glared in her eyes as she ran back to the truck. Myriads of people in Wyoming drove pickup trucks. Hopefully this person lived in Fort Lob, someone she knew.

The driver's door opened, and Derek Brandt stepped down from the cab. Wearing a Western shirt, jeans, and a white cowboy hat, he looked like an authentic cowboy. "Hi, Cheyenne. Need help?"

Relief poured through her, and she hadn't realized until that moment how tense she was. "Oh Derek, am I glad to see you!" She laughed. If she had to be stranded, at least she was rescued by the most handsome man in the West. "My car died. Could you give me a lift into town?"

"Sure." He pulled a flashlight from under his front seat, then walked around to the front of her car. "What's wrong with it?" He leaned over to peer down, shining the light on different parts of the engine.

"A lot of steam poured out when I opened the hood." Standing beside him, a quiet peace filled her. *Thank You, Lord, for sending Derek!*

"Must be the radiator." He straightened and snapped off the light. "Guess you'll need to be towed."

"Could you tow my car, Derek?"

He tapped the flashlight in his palm. "I would, but I lent my chains to Miguel, one of our hired hands. Call Tom

Shoemacher when you get home. He'll tow it to his garage."
Derek walked back to his truck and motioned for her to
follow. "Hop in."

Cheyenne grabbed her purse and notebook from her car,
then got in on the passenger side of his pickup. "Thanks for
the lift." She closed the door.

"Not a problem. Why were you way out here tonight?"

She settled on the seat as he pulled around her car and
headed down the road. "I'm taking a class in Lusk."

Derek frowned. "What for?"

"Well. . ." How could she tell Derek she was trying to learn
beauty tips to go along with her weight-loss program? "I'm
learning the art of applying makeup." Stopping, she pressed
her lips together. *I'm doing this for you, mister!*

His eyes roved her face before his gaze caught hers. For a
brief moment, a sudden chemistry arced between them.

Clearing his throat, Derek looked back at the road. "Your
makeup looks good enough to me."

"See? I'm doing it right."

He chuckled.

She sank back against the seat. *What did that look mean?*
A touch of nerves hit her stomach. Here they were, alone
in Derek's truck, but he didn't seem to want to deepen
their friendship. A tiny sigh escaped her lips. "Tomorrow
evening is my makeup test, and Tonya agreed to be my
model, although she said she might be late."

"How are you gonna get there? I doubt if Tom will have
your car fixed by tomorrow night."

"Oh." Cheyenne bit her lower lip. She hadn't thought of
that. "Maybe I can borrow my dad's car if he doesn't mind
being stranded at the store all evening."

"Hey, no worries. I'll drive you to Lusk."

Cheyenne raised her eyebrows. "But that's way out of your
way."

"My schedule is flexible. Besides"—he grinned at her—
"you went out of your way when I was sick last week, so it's

the least I can do to pay you back."

"You don't have to pay me back, Derek, but I do need a ride." And it would be more time spent with him. She hadn't seen much of him lately. "Okay, I'll take you up on your offer."

He nodded. "What time should I pick you up tomorrow night? Six thirty?"

"Sounds good." In fact, the whole plan sounded better than good.

Now if only Tom Shoemacher would keep her car for a while!

❧

On Friday evening, Derek sat on a folding chair beside Cheyenne at The Maximum Cut in Lusk. He watched a girl with a brown ponytail apply makeup to the pasty face of another girl, but she wasn't the only student taking the makeup test. All five beautician chairs in the room were occupied, with each student industriously applying makeup to her model.

The teacher, with fluffy brown hair piled on top of her head and shaved up the back, walked around and wrote notes about each girl's demonstration on a clipboard.

With a sigh, Derek folded his arms. Too bad he hadn't brought a book to read.

Sitting next to Cheyenne, he could almost feel the tension radiating from her. Tonya had not shown up yet. Cheyenne had tried to call her several times, but her cell phone wouldn't connect.

Leave it to Tonya to be late.

Cheyenne's phone chirped. "Finally!" She flipped it open. "Tonya, where are you?" She listened for a few minutes.

The girl with the ponytail finished her test, and she and the other girl took seats on the folding chairs. Derek had to admit, the model's pasty face had been transformed.

Closing her phone, Cheyenne turned to him. "Tonya can't come. Murray's mom had a setback at the nursing home, and they're on their way to Douglas right now."

Derek frowned. "That's not good."

"Yeah, I hope she's okay. But now I don't have a model."

The teacher turned toward her. "Cheyenne, are you ready? We have an empty chair."

Standing, Cheyenne twisted her hands. "I'm sorry, Mrs. Bartlett. My model won't be able to make it, so I guess I can't take the test." Her shoulders drooped.

Derek glanced around. In the quiet room, the other girls had all stopped their work to stare at Cheyenne with their painted eyes. Had he and Cheyenne driven all this way for nothing?

He stood. "I'll be your model."

Cheyenne's jaw dropped, and several of the students tittered.

He turned to the group. "Hey, I have a face, don't I?" He rubbed his chin. "I even shaved this morning."

His words caused more giggles, and the teacher smiled.

Cheyenne placed her hand on his arm. "You wouldn't mind, Derek?"

He shrugged. "Why not? Let's get this show on the road."

"Thanks." Her dimples creased as she smiled up at him.

He nodded, thinking once again how pretty she was, then took a seat in the chair. Cheyenne threw the cape around his shoulders and snapped it at the back of his neck.

She selected a small brown bottle from the counter under the mirror. "I have to test the foundation shade underneath your jawline first and blend it into your neck to see if it's the right color." Opening the bottle, she dumped some tan liquid on a wedge-shaped sponge.

Derek lifted his chin as she dabbed his neck.

"This color is perfect." Cheyenne dabbed some more on the sponge. "Now I'll apply it evenly to your face. I have to blend it carefully so there's no smudge line." Her voice dropped to a whisper. "That's the hard part."

He tried to relax, closing his eyes as she swabbed his face with even strokes. He was only doing this for her. But one thought kept running through his mind.

I'm going to look like a girl.

⋆

Cheyenne stepped back. "That's the last step, and your makeup is complete." She smiled at Derek, who now looked more beautiful than handsome with his outlined, dark-lashed eyes and pink cheeks.

A smattering of applause echoed through the room from the other girls. They had finished their tests, and for the past five minutes they surrounded Cheyenne. It was a little nerve-racking, but Cheyenne had a feeling they wanted to see what this hot guy looked like in makeup.

Derek glanced back at the mirror and then pinned Cheyenne with his gaze. "Now we need a demonstration of how to take makeup off."

Everyone laughed, and Mrs. Bartlett nodded. "That's a good idea, Cheyenne. I'll give you a bonus point for showing us how to remove it."

"Okay." She smiled as she picked up the bottle of oil-free makeup remover from the counter. "First I'll remove your eye makeup."

"Amen to that," Derek muttered as he closed his eyes.

Cheyenne applied the remover carefully, not wanting to get any in his eyes. She'd be forever grateful to Derek for volunteering to be her model. But the bonus for her was being able to touch every millimeter of his face—smoothing foundation over his skin, outlining his dark eyes, gazing at his handsome features.

She was going to keep working and praying to win his hand—by the end of this year.

⋆

"I appreciate the ride." Cheyenne touched the passenger door handle of Derek's truck as it idled in her driveway. She wished she could sit here and talk with him awhile but it was getting late, and he always got up early to care for the animals at the ranch. "Thanks for being my model tonight.

You really went the second mile—literally on the road as well as for my makeup test." She laughed at her own joke.

He grinned. "Glad to do it. We make a good team."

"Yes, we do." Smiling, she pulled the handle. The door popped open, and the truck's inside light came on.

"Hey, if you need a ride to the bowling activity on Tuesday night, let me know."

"Okay, thanks." She looked back at him then frowned. "You still have a spot of mascara under your eye."

"I do?" He studied his reflection in the rearview mirror. "Yeah, so I do."

Cheyenne rummaged in her purse. "Let me clean that off." She pulled out a tissue.

Derek threw his arm across the back of the bench seat and leaned toward her.

She dabbed the tissue under his eye, feeling his gaze on her. Their faces were so close—a little tingle went up her spine at his nearness. She wiped the tissue under his lashes one last time, wishing she could stay a few more minutes, but her job was done. "There, that's better." She looked into his eyes.

His gaze held hers. "Much better." His eyes dipped down to her lips.

Cheyenne caught a quick breath. He was going to kiss her!

But Derek suddenly cleared his throat and sat back. "Thanks." Placing a fist against his mouth, he coughed. "Uh, guess I'll see you Sunday at church."

"Yeah." She fumbled to push the door open. "See you later." Jumping out of the pickup, she closed the door.

He backed out of the driveway then took off down the road. An aura of sadness enveloped her like a shroud. *He almost kissed me!* But something stopped him.

What was it?

❧

Whew! That was close.

Derek hit the steering wheel with his fist as he drove out of town. If Cheyenne hadn't given that little gasp, he would have pulled her in his arms and kissed her. Whatever had possessed him? He knew God's will. *Single for the Lord.*

He huffed out a breath. He would not mess up again.

But he had already offered Cheyenne a ride on Tuesday night to the bowling alley, so he'd have to give her a lift if her car was still in the shop.

He thought back to those few moments in the truck as she wiped the tissue under his eye. She was so close he could actually feel her softness. And some type of awareness crackled between them. But why had he suddenly turned into a love-struck teenager?

Crazy.

With a shake of his head, he stepped on the gas and roared down the road. He had to make sure that didn't happen again.

five

On Tuesday afternoon, the bell over the door to the Fort Lob Post Office signaled a customer.

Cheyenne put down the mail she was sorting and walked out from the back room to stand behind the counter. "May I help you?"

A tall, thin cowboy removed his black hat, revealing a thatch of brown hair. His tanned face had a weathered look. "Hello there, ma'am. I'd like to secure a post office box."

"Okay." Cheyenne pulled a form from under the counter. "Just fill this out." With a smile, she handed it to him.

He pulled a pen from his inside jacket pocket and leaned over the counter to fill in the boxes.

She waited a few minutes, watching his large, tanned hands. Those hands were definitely used to work. "You must be new in town."

"Yep." He had a deep voice. "Just bought the ranch that was for sale on Antelope Road."

"Oh—the old Dudley place." Cheyenne's memory conjured up images of the elderly couple who had died. Their children had been trying to sell the ranch for years. "That ranch is next to The Rocking B, owned by Jake Brandt. Have you met the Brandts yet?"

"Nope." Leaning over the counter, he glanced up at her with his brown eyes. "I haven't met a single soul in Fort Lob. Even the Realtor was from out of town."

Cheyenne grinned. "Well, you've met me." She held out her right hand. "I'm Cheyenne Wilkins. Welcome to Fort Lob."

He straightened and shook her hand. "Glad to meet you, Mrs. Wilkins."

"It's *Miss*, but please call me Cheyenne. Everyone does."

A slow smile spread across his face, crinkling the corners of his eyes. "Cheyenne. A pretty name for a pretty lady."

Her heart skipped a beat. "Thank you." She looked down, rather embarrassed to be called a "pretty lady." But she couldn't help noticing how his smile transformed his features. He looked around forty years old and his skin looked like tanned leather, but that smile made him handsome.

He pushed the form toward her. "Rex Pierson. Moving from Montana, and I'm gonna pepper my new ranch with beef cattle and buffalo."

Cheyenne glanced up. "So you're raising them for meat?"

"Yes, ma'am. I mean, *Cheyenne*." Rex grinned.

She smiled back then looked down at the form. "Would you rather pay for your post office box for six months or for a year?"

They transacted business, and Cheyenne showed Rex where his box was located along the wall. When they were finished, he thanked her and turned toward the door. She walked back to the counter.

"By the way. . ." Rex stopped. "Is there a good restaurant in town where I could have supper?"

"We have two good restaurants." She joined him at the glass door and pointed outside. "The Cattlemen's Diner is located across the street. That would be my first choice for supper." She pointed to the left down the road. "Then there's the Trailblazer Café. That's a good choice for breakfast or lunch."

With a nod, he squinted as he looked out the door. "Another thing I'm looking for is a good church." His brown eyes turned to her. "Any around here? I'm looking for one that has a Bible study or prayer service on Wednesday night."

Cheyenne's lips parted. "You must be a Christian!"

"Yep." His smile deepened the wrinkle lines on his face. "Blood-washed, bought, and on my way to heaven."

Wow. "That's great! My church has a prayer service on Wednesday, and services on Sunday, too."

"Where's it located?"

She gave him directions, pointing out the door.

"Thank you, Cheyenne. You've been most helpful." He donned his cowboy hat.

She watched him amble across the street and enter the diner. Her heart warmed at the thought of meeting another Christian, one who wasn't afraid to share his testimony. Then she thought of what he had called her. *Pretty lady.* With a smile, she shook her head. Her thoughts wandered to Grandmother's will and Derek Brandt. Did he think she was a pretty lady?

All weekend she had ruminated on that intimate moment with him in his truck.

The near kiss that turned into a near miss.

She didn't tell anyone what happened, not even Callie. Now if Derek had actually kissed her, Callie would have been the first person to find out.

What went wrong?

A definite chemistry had hung between them in that moment, and he must have felt it, too. Why had he suddenly gotten cold feet?

She would probably never know.

૨ა

That evening Cheyenne leaned over to tie her bowling shoes, then cuffed the bottom edges of her jeans and flattened them out. The noise of conversation and laughter, along with the clatter of bowling pins, surrounded her. Only seven members of the Single Servings showed up for the bowling activity, and they claimed two lanes. Cheyenne was on a lane with Matthew Werth and Derek.

Sitting up, she glanced around the bowling alley. In the next lane, Corey Henning already stood behind the line and released his ball down the lane with a tight spin. The pins crashed in a strike. With a whoop, Corey turned toward the three people sitting behind him—Laurie Smullens, whom he was dating, Reed Dickens, and Horace Frankenberg.

Derek sat to Cheyenne's left in a plastic chair, tying his shoes. He stood. "Now to find a good ball. It's times like this when I wish I owned one." He grinned at Matthew who stood by the ball return.

"Yep." Matthew pulled a red bowling ball from his bag. He held up his gloved hand. "I'm trying this Super-Flex 3000 wrist support glove. I'm hoping it will add a few points to my game." He bent over the hand dryer.

Cheyenne rolled her eyes as she stood. "I'll go with you, Derek." Since her car was still at Tom's shop, Derek had driven her to the bowling alley and acted as if nothing had happened between them on Friday. But she wanted something to happen. Tonight.

I'll stick to him like gum on his shoe!

The conditions of Grandmother's will lingered. She needed to make every day count.

Behind him, she ascended the three steps from their lane. "I didn't even know they made bowling gloves."

Derek turned. "Of course they do. That's why the two middle fingers are missing." He walked beside her to the ball rack. "What kind of ball do you want?"

"I need a light ball, but I can never find one that fits."

He hefted a blue ball then put it down. "Are you a good bowler, Cheyenne?"

"No!" She laughed. "My highest score of all time is 83. I'll be lucky if I can stay out of the gutter."

He grinned. "Just so your life doesn't end up in the gutter."

"Oh thanks a lot." She smiled, loving it when he teased her.

Derek hefted a yellow ball then handed it to her. "Try this one—it's light."

Cheyenne glanced at the tiny finger holes and shook her head. "My fingers will get stuck." She sighed as she set the ball down. "That's my problem. The bigger the finger holes, the heavier the ball. I suppose the reasoning is that a bowler with big fingers must be strong." *And how am I supposed to lose weight in my fingers?*

Derek twisted a purple ball on the rack so the holes were on top. "Here. Try this one."

As she took it, the door to the bowling alley opened. Bruce MacKinnon and Aggie Collingsworth walked in.

It must be true that opposites attract. Cheyenne hid a smile as the pair walked toward them. Bruce, a dignified Scotsman whose speech still held a slight brogue, was dating Aggie, an overweight down-home gal from Texas, complete with southern accent.

A short young woman walked beside Bruce. A pair of jeans clung to her thin hips, and long red hair flowed over the shoulders of her jade T-shirt. With bright eyes and a pretty smile, she was cute.

And tiny.

That girl would never get *her* fingers stuck in a bowling ball.

Aggie nodded at Derek and Cheyenne. "Howdy, y'all. Having fun at this bowling shindig?"

Cheyenne smiled. "Hi! Are you guys joining us tonight?" Aggie was in their Sunday school class, but Bruce taught an adult class, and the girl looked like she might be in high school.

Bruce motioned to the women beside him. "Agatha wants to go shopping in Lusk, but my granddaughter, Kandi, would like to join you in the activity." He looked at Derek. "Is that all right?"

Derek shrugged. "Sure. The more the merrier." He extended his hand toward the girl. "Derek Brandt. Glad to meet you."

She shook his hand. "I'm Kandi MacKinnon."

Since Cheyenne held a bowling ball, she just nodded at the girl. "I'm Cheyenne. Welcome to the party."

Kandi had obviously mastered beauty secrets. The makeup on her smooth face was perfect, with the green eye shadow bringing out the green in her eyes. Her eyelashes were thick.

Bruce smiled at his granddaughter. "Kandi attends a Christian college in California, but she's staying with me this summer. She'll be in your Sunday school class, Derek."

"That's great." Smiling, he took a step toward her. "What year in college?"

She looked up at him, returning his smile. "I'll be a sophomore in the fall."

Derek thumbed back at their lane. "You can bowl with me. There's only three on our lane."

"Thanks."

Cheyenne cocked an eyebrow. Derek seemed entirely too interested in Kandi MacKinnon. The girl couldn't be more than five foot three—a whole foot shorter than Derek—but she gazed up at him with a dazzling smile as they walked back to the lane. Bruce and Aggie departed, which left Cheyenne standing alone by the ball rack.

Derek was just being friendly. Yeah, that was it. After all, he was the teacher of the Single Servings. He had to be friendly.

As long as he's not too friendly.

&

Derek relaxed in the plastic chair as he watched Kandi release her ball into the lane. She was so pretty! And he couldn't believe how athletic she was, with perfect bowling form. Already, on the seventh frame, her score was 149. Derek only had 116, and Cheyenne trailed behind with a mere 52 points. Of course Matthew, the pro, had a leading score of 218.

Kandi waited as her ball quickly spun down the lane. Upon impact, all the pins succumbed with a crash, and she whirled around, raising both hands in the air. "Strike!"

Derek grinned. "Great job!" He glanced at her lithe figure as she walked toward him. *She's so small!* He loved her red hair, and he'd already christened her *the little red-haired girl,* like Charlie Brown's girlfriend in *Peanuts.*

He wanted to get to know Kandi MacKinnon.

For a moment his conscience struck him. What about remaining single to serve the Lord? But was that what the

Lord really wanted him to do?

"I thought that was going to be a split." She took the seat beside him.

He grinned. "You're a good bowler, Kandi."

She returned a shy smile. "Thanks."

He gazed at her pretty green eyes, her soft red hair. *She's so pretty.* Maybe he should ask her out.

❧

On the way home from the bowling alley, Cheyenne stared out the passenger window of Derek's pickup, even though it was pitch-black, and tried to tune out Derek's voice. *Please give me patience, Lord!*

This night had not turned out as she had hoped.

When Bruce and Aggie came by to pick up Kandi at the beginning of their third game, Derek volunteered to take her home—which meant, of course, that Cheyenne had to ride with them. Now they bumped along in his truck, with Kandi in the middle of the cab sandwiched between Cheyenne and Derek. The girl didn't say much, but she sure smiled a lot, mainly at Derek who had never talked so much in his life. All Cheyenne could do was sit there and grit her teeth.

He pulled into her driveway. "Here you are, Cheyenne."

Of course he would drop her off first.

She opened the passenger door, and the inside light popped on. *Déjà vu.* Was Derek thinking about what happened between them last Friday night? She climbed out. "Thanks for the ride."

"Anytime, Cheyenne."

She looked back as she closed the door. Kandi, who had barely moved two inches away from him, smiled at her.

Cheyenne trudged to the house, not looking back as the truck pulled out and roared down the street. With a sigh, she crossed the porch to the front door, which was illuminated by the porch light.

Stopping at the door, she bowed her head until it touched the wood. For ten years she had thought she would someday marry Derek Brandt. He was perfect for her—calm in every situation where she was emotional, staying in the background when she liked to be out front.

Well, he's not the only man in the world. Perhaps God had someone else in mind—someone who would be even more perfect. Someone who would complete her.

"Lord," she whispered. "Please show me who that someone is. Show me Your will."

She took a deep breath. God already had her future all worked out. But would it happen in time? Would she be able to fulfill the conditions of Grandmother's will?

She walked to the edge of the porch and looked up at the shiny white moon high above. "All I need is a man, Lord!"

࣪ࣂ

On Wednesday afternoon, Cheyenne walked from the garage to the house, glad her Dart was back from Tom's shop and thankful she didn't have to depend on Derek Brandt to cart her around. Now to get out of her postal uniform and eat something before the prayer service at church. Dad wouldn't be home until after eight o'clock when he closed the store for the evening.

Entering the house, she pushed the back door shut. Marshal greeted her with a bark.

"Hey, Marsh!" She patted the collie's tan head then bent down and let him lick her face. She relished his affectionate greeting. "Okay, Marshal. That's good." She laughed. "I guess you missed me today, huh?"

He answered her question with another bark then turned in a circle and sat down by the back door.

Cheyenne placed her hands on her hips. "Sorry, I'm not taking you for a walk. That's Dad's job. I'm planning to eat something and go to church."

Dad always took Marshal out around ten o'clock at night, and Cheyenne was glad she didn't have to walk the dog. She hated exercise in any form, even walking.

She strolled back to her bedroom and stopped in the doorway. *What a mess!*

A corner of her tiger poster, which had been hanging between the windows since high school, peeled away from the wall. Piles of clothes littered the chair, and her bed had not been made since she changed the sheets three days ago.

With a sigh, she walked inside, mentally comparing this room to Derek's. *Why can't I keep my room neat?*

She plucked her jeans from the pile on the chair. They were still cuffed from bowling last night. With a sigh, she sat down on her bed, reliving those memories. If only Kandi MacKinnon hadn't shown up! She was such a good bowler.

And my bowling was awful!

But what really bothered Cheyenne was Derek's reaction to Kandi. He seemed more infatuated with her as the evening wore on. "Well!" Cheyenne shook her jeans at Marshal, who had padded into the bedroom. "I don't need him! I'm going to lose weight, and just maybe I'll find another man."

Yeah right. Her shoulders slumped. Maybe God did have another man for her, but Derek had always been her number-one candidate for marriage. After all these years, it was depressing that another girl had caught his attention. And a tiny, cute girl at that.

Marsh sat down and thumped his tail against the floor. His almond-shaped eyes gazed at her as his tongue hung out in a pant.

Grabbing a women's magazine from her nightstand, Cheyenne leaned back against the pillows. She glanced at the thin model on the cover and read the titles of the articles listed there. Her eyes stopped at one. "Walking Off the Pounds."

Biting her lower lip, she glanced at Marshal. What better way to lose weight than to take the dog for a walk every day?

With a sigh, she looked at the clock on the dresser. It was only 5:22.

She had plenty of time.

six

After the waiter took their order, Derek gazed across the table at Kandi MacKinnon. The elegant Four Seasons restaurant in Cheyenne, Wyoming, was bustling with customers on this Friday evening, but he only saw her. They sat at a small table for two at the back of the dining room, and Derek couldn't have asked for a more perfect spot.

He raised his eyebrows. "All you ordered was a salad? You're not watching your weight, are you?" He winked, letting her know he was kidding.

"No." Her face tinged pink, adding to the blush that blended in perfectly with her foundation. Thanks to Cheyenne, Derek knew all about makeup.

She shrugged. "I guess I'm not that hungry."

Is she nervous? Derek had to admit he was nervous himself. This was only the second time in his life he had purposely asked a girl on a date because he wanted to. The moment he saw Kandi in church Wednesday night, he asked if she would go to dinner with him on Friday.

Tonight she had dressed up in a green sleeveless dress, and her freckled arms looked athletic with firm muscles. It was amazing how attracted he was to *the little red-haired girl.* Maybe Mom was right—he should get married.

That thought *really* made him nervous.

He glanced around at the other patrons of the Four Seasons, other couples at other tables having intimate conversations. Looking back at Kandi, he gazed at her pretty green eyes. "So. . .you have three more years in college. What are you majoring in, Kandi?"

"English literature." She smoothed the napkin lying beside her plate.

"So. . .English." He cleared his throat. Why did he keep saying *so*? "What are you going to do when you graduate?"

"I might go on for my master's degree."

"You're not going to become one of those professional students, are you?" He grinned.

That pink hue crept to her face once more, and she shook her head. "No." Her fingers started picking at the edge of the napkin.

Derek drew in a silent sigh, wishing Kandi would expand her short English sentences. On the way to the restaurant, he had done most of the talking, telling her about his degree in range management from the University of Montana and about his family. She just listened. How could he get to know her if she didn't talk?

"My sister, Callie, majored in English. She worked as a librarian until she got married. Now she and her husband are building a museum for our town."

"Oh."

"Would you be interested in becoming a librarian someday?"

"I don't know." She looked down at the tablecloth. "I might."

Taking a deep breath, he tried again. "Tell me about your family, Kandi." He sat back. *I've got you there!* She couldn't tell him about her family in a three-word sentence.

"I have a mom and dad, a sister, and a brother." She leaned forward. "We've lived in Salt Lake City since I was four years old. My dad was transferred there."

"I see." He nodded, hoping it would encourage her to keep talking. "What does your dad do?"

As she answered, Derek felt like he was playing Twenty Questions. Was Kandi always this quiet? Maybe she was shy.

Cheyenne's face popped into his mind. Now there was a girl who could talk! For a moment, he wished she was the one sitting across from him. But why was he even attempting to date a pretty girl? Didn't the Lord want him to remain single in order to serve Him?

No wonder this date with Kandi was going nowhere.

٭

Cheyenne tried to control her breathing as she opened the back door. "Okay, Marshal, that was our exercise for tonight." She was panting more than he was.

The collie waited while she unhooked his leash. Then he lay down on his doggy bed by the back door.

"My sentiments exactly, Marsh." Heaving out a breath, she walked into her bedroom and threw herself across the bed, facedown. *I must have lost fifty pounds!*

She'd been walking Marshal every evening for three days, and she'd eaten nothing but fruit and salads, plus some egg whites for protein. So far, according to the bathroom scale, she had lost exactly two pounds. Two pounds! So on her "walk" with Marshal tonight, she started jogging.

Mistake!

She was still trying to catch her breath when her cell phone rang.

With a groan, she sat up and swiped her phone off the dresser. She glanced at the caller's number before flipping it open. "Hi, Callie." She sighed. "What's up?"

"Hi! You sound kind of down."

Cheyenne flopped to her back. "I just got back from jogging with Marshal."

"Jogging? You?" The sound of a chuckle escaped over the phone.

"It's not funny! Marshal and I are trying to lose weight, you know."

"Hmm. . .I didn't realize he was overweight."

"He's not." Cheyenne sighed. "But you know what? I've lost two pounds in the last three days."

"That's great! I'm proud of you, Chey. Keep up the exercise with Marshal, and someday you'll be thinner than Tonya."

"Oh sure." Cheyenne laughed. "What can I do for you, girlfriend?"

Callie paused. "I hate to give you bad news when you're

tired, but I thought you should know about this."

"Bad news?" Cheyenne sat up. "What happened? Did someone die? It's not Murray's mother, is it?"

"No, nothing like that. In fact, his mom is doing a lot better."

"Oh, that's good." Cheyenne breathed out. "So what's the bad news?"

"It's about Derek. I was talking to Mom on the phone just now, and she told me Derek took Kandi MacKinnon to the Four Seasons tonight."

"What!" Cheyenne jumped to her feet. "He asked her out? You've got to be kidding!"

"Would I joke about a thing like that?" Callie paused. "Derek is finally dating someone of his own volition, and to be honest, I'm brokenhearted. I had high hopes for you and him."

With a moan, Cheyenne sank down to the bed. "I've lost Derek for sure. How can I compete with that teeny-weeny girl who has zero fat on her teeny-weeny body?"

"Chey. . ."

"It's true! There is no way I can compete with her." Cheyenne walked to the full-length mirror. Looking at her almost-six-foot pudgy self decked out in sweats, she grimaced. "If I ever succeed in getting married, it will be to a man whose sole passion is to fall in love with a big, fat woman."

"Chey, Derek likes you. He's comfortable around you."

"But not in love." She dropped down to her bed. "I'm thinking of doing something different, Callie. Something radical."

"Oh?"

"Yep. I'm moving to Colorado."

"What? You can't move! You've been my best friend since first grade."

"Life changes, Callie. I'm thinking about Loveland." She smiled. "Isn't that a great name? That's where I'll find the love of my life." She lifted up a quick prayer, asking God to make it so.

"But that's so far away."

"Not that far, Callie. I already put in for a transfer at the post office, but I'm also looking at other jobs."

"You're really serious, aren't you?"

Cheyenne ignored the question. "Remember that makeup class I took a couple weeks ago? I'm applying for a job at Hallie's Beauty Supply Shoppe in Loveland. It's a new store, and their grand opening is next month." Her heart leaped. "Can you imagine? I took that class just for myself, but the Lord knew that certificate would help me get this job. It looks like He's working everything out for good."

"Please don't move, Cheyenne." Callie's voice had a whine tucked inside it. "Don't give up on Derek yet. You two would make such a great couple. You're perfect for each other in every way. And besides, I've always wanted you to be my sister-in-law."

A tiny flicker ignited in Cheyenne's heart, but she snuffed it out. Why should she hold out for Derek Brandt? "It's no use, Callie. I'm just one of Derek's many friends—no one special."

"That's not true. You two are the best of friends."

"Give it up, Callie. Derek has his eyes on Kandi, and the Lord has someone else in mind for me. At least, I hope so." *And I need to meet him soon!*

If only she could tell Callie about Grandmother's will.

"Well. . .okay. But I'm going to keep praying about you and Derek." Callie paused. "Remember how you encouraged me last summer when I was ready to give up on Lane?"

Cheyenne thought back. "You said you didn't have peace about dating him."

"I didn't! But you thought we were perfect for each other, and you told me to trust the Lord to work things out. And He did!"

A lone tear rolled down Cheyenne's cheek, but she brushed it away.

"The Lord can do the same for you and Derek." The

sound of static filled the phone. "I have to go, Chey. Talk to you later."

"Bye, Callie."

Dropping her phone in her purse, Cheyenne closed her eyes. She *was* excited about moving, but if Derek gave any indication that he wanted to marry her, she would rather stay in Fort Lob. Her shoulders slumped as all the air escaped from her lungs. She couldn't believe Derek had asked Kandi out.

So much for trying to win his hand.

❧

The stars shone in the dark sky as Derek drove his pickup to the front of Bruce MacKinnon's house. He stopped beside the front porch where the porch light cast a warm glow. "Here we are."

Kandi touched the handle of the passenger door. "Thanks, Derek."

"Let me get that for you." He walked around the front of the truck and opened her door then grabbed her elbow to help her down.

The front door of the house opened, and Bruce stuck his head outside. "I wondered when you two would get home. I'm glad it's not too late."

Derek grinned at him. "I brought her right home, Bruce."

"That you did." He opened the screen door wider as Kandi ascended the porch steps. "Why don't you come in and set a spell, as Agatha would say."

"Okay." Derek climbed the porch steps and walked into the house where the air-conditioning made a noticeable difference. He didn't want to "set a spell." Kandi had barely said two complete sentences on the hour-long drive home from the big city so he had talked for both of them.

It was exhausting.

Bruce motioned toward the blue and white plaid sofa where his granddaughter was sitting in the middle. "Have a seat. Can I get you something to drink?"

"No thanks." Derek eased down next to Kandi and sank

into the comfortable cushions. He hadn't been to Bruce MacKinnon's house for years. A blue braided rug partially covered the polished wooden floor, and several lighthouses decorated the fireplace mantelpiece.

Bruce faced them as he took a seat in a wooden rocking chair. "It certainly was warm out today."

Derek nodded. "It hit 101 degrees this afternoon. Hope it cools off, especially during the last week of July. Dad and I plan to be in Cheyenne for the rodeo."

"Ah! You must be referring to Cheyenne Frontier Days."

"Yep." Derek grinned. "Time for cowboys to get down and dirty."

"Cowboys?" Beside him, Kandi perked up. "What rodeo is this?"

He glanced at her. "Cowboys call it 'The Daddy of 'Em All.' It's been held every July since 1897. They do cattle roping, barrel racing, and bull riding, among other things. They even have pancake breakfasts and parades. It's a huge event, lasting ten or twelve days."

"Wow." Her pretty eyes stared into his. "Are you doing any cattle roping?"

"No." He grinned. "I'm a sheep rancher, not a cowboy."

Bruce leaned back in his rocker. "How many days are you going, Derek?"

"Dad and I go every day except Sunday. We love watching the cowboy contests. My mom and sisters only attend one day. They like to see what people are wearing." Derek laughed. "You can tell a city slicker in cowboy getup a mile away."

"Aye." Bruce chuckled. "That's one reason I don't go. I feel out of my element."

Derek raised his eyebrows. "You're not going this year?"

Bruce shook his head. "I never do. Once, about fifteen years ago, I attended the rodeo. That was enough for me."

Kandi folded her arms. "Well you'll have to go this year, Grandpa. I want to see it, especially the cowboys roping cattle. I'd really like to see a parade, too. Sounds awesome."

She smiled at Derek.

That's the most I heard her talk all night! "The parades are held three or four days in downtown Cheyenne."

"Do they have floats?"

"Yep. Floats, marching bands, antique cars. It's great, especially if the weather is good."

"And what about the pancake breakfast?"

"They have three free breakfasts on Monday, Wednesday, and Friday during the last week."

"Awesome." She turned to her grandfather. "You have to take me one of those days, Grandpa."

Bruce stopped rocking. "Sorry to disappoint, dear girl, but I can't stand out in the hot sun all day. Your grandfather is too old for that kind of thing."

"You can go with our family, Kandi." Derek hastened to emphasize the others. "My mom and sisters hang out together, and they would love to show you around." Looking at Bruce, he frowned as a thought popped into his head. "I assume Callie and Tonya will go with us. This is the first summer that both of them are married."

Bruce nodded. "They'll drag their men with them, I'm sure, although Murray was on patrol duty last July. He might be on duty again this year."

Derek rubbed his chin. "Yeah, I remember seeing Twitch in his uniform."

"Twitch?" Kandi raised her eyebrows.

"My brother-in-law, Murray Twichell."

"That's his name?" She shook her head. "Poor guy."

Derek frowned. "I never thought a thing about Murray's name. I've known the Twichells since I was born."

"Aye, a name becomes familiar." Bruce looked at his granddaughter. "Of course, not everyone has a great last name like MacKinnon."

"It's the best!" Kandi laughed. "I'm proud to have Scottish blood running through my veins."

Derek glanced at her, thankful she was finally contributing

to the conversation. Perhaps shyness had been the culprit on their date. But it didn't matter. He should have listened to his conscience in the first place.

Dating and I just don't get along.

seven

At nine forty-five on Monday night, Cheyenne glanced up from the book she was reading as Dad's voice filled the house.

"Come on, Marshal. Time for our walk, boy."

Marshal barked several times by the back door.

"Cheyenne!" Dad bellowed. "Marsh and I are leaving!"

"Okay, Dad." She had read the same paragraph three times and still didn't know what it said.

She waited to hear the back door open, but it didn't happen. Instead Dad walked to the living room, leading Marsh. "Hey, do you want to go with us?"

She raised her eyebrows. "On the walk?"

"Yeah. It's a beautiful evening. You could get some exercise."

With a sigh, she laid aside her book. Even her dad was telling her she needed to lose weight. "Sure, I'll go with you."

"We can talk. Seems like I never see you anymore, baby girl."

They left the house, and Cheyenne fell into step beside him on the smooth sidewalk. For a big man, he walked fast. Marshal trotted at his side with the leash limp in Dad's hand.

Cheyenne breathed in the warm night air. Every minute or so, they passed under a street lamp, the light spreading a yellow circle around them before they entered the darkness again. A thin sliver of moon peeked through the trees.

"Where are we going?" *I can't believe I'm not winded yet.* Maybe she was in better shape than she thought.

"I always go to the park." Dad looked down at the dog. "It's peaceful at this time of night, and Marshal enjoys the scenery."

She grinned. "Marsh would enjoy the slums of Calcutta."

They turned right on Pronghorn Avenue and passed the Elks Lodge, which was dark. Soon the houses ended, and a glow of lights signaled the park's entrance. Inside, a maze of sidewalks skirted around trees, benches, and light posts. Several other people strolled the sidewalks, and they greeted them as they passed.

"You're right, Dad. This is peaceful." Cheyenne took in a deep breath. "I should do more walking at night."

"Not without Marshal or me." Dad cocked an eyebrow at her. "A young woman shouldn't be out by herself, even in a safe town like Fort Lob."

"I'll remember that, Dad, especially when I move."

He grabbed her arm, forcing her to stop and face him. "You're moving, baby girl?"

Oops! How had she let that slip? She looked up into his blue eyes, knowing she had to tell him eventually. "I guess I didn't tell you my plans."

"No."

"I need a change in my life, Dad." She began walking at a more leisurely pace. "I'm thinking of moving out of the house."

Dad strolled beside her. "It's about time you became independent. I suppose you want to buy your own place in Fort Lob."

They passed a park bench illuminated by a lamppost. "Not in Fort Lob. I'd like to move to Loveland."

"In Colorado?" He stopped again, and his voice echoed through the park. "That's crazy!"

"Dad!" Holding up her hands, Cheyenne almost whispered. "Keep your voice down."

"I am keeping my voice down," he said, just as loud as before. "Why do you want to move to Colorado?"

She sighed. "I feel stuck, Dad. Maybe if I settle somewhere different, I can meet a new guy."

Rex Pierson's handsome face popped into her mind. He

came to the post office every day to check his box, and he always greeted her. Sometimes they talked for ten or fifteen minutes before he left, and she enjoyed the conversation. But he was just being friendly.

Besides, he's too old for me.

Dad pursed his lips, then turned and strode down the sidewalk with Marsh trotting beside him. Cheyenne caught up, knowing better than to interrupt Dad's thoughts. She prayed he wasn't offended that she wanted to leave but would instead give his blessing.

After circling the park and coming back to the same spot, Dad motioned to the bench under the lamppost. "Let's sit down."

They settled on the bench with Marshal sitting at their feet. He panted as he surveyed the area, and Cheyenne reached down to fondle his ear. *No worries for you, Marsh.*

Dad placed his hefty arm on the back of the bench behind her. "I assume you've prayed about this?"

She nodded. "I already applied for a couple jobs in Loveland, and I feel good about it. Maybe this is God's will for me."

"When do you plan to move?"

She lifted one shoulder in a shrug. "As soon as I get a job."

Dad grunted then looked her in the eye. "You'll have to join a good church when you move."

He was giving his blessing! *Thank You, Lord!* "I know the Lord will lead me to the right church, but do you think I'll make it, Dad? I have less than two years."

Dad squeezed her shoulder. "We'll have to keep praying, baby girl." He paused. "God's ways are not our ways. Maybe He doesn't want you to have that money."

"But Dad. . ." Her eyes widened. "Four million dollars!"

He gave her a sad smile. "We've lived without it all these years, and the Lord has always provided." A muscle in his cheek jumped. " 'Course, I'd hate for George Sommers to inherit that money. He'll just sink it into his casino."

She grit her teeth. "That will not happen, Dad. But that's why I have to move and meet someone different. No one in Fort Lob is standing at my door begging to marry me."

"Truth to tell, I always figured you'd end up with Derek, but I guess your interest in him died out."

"I'm still interested. *His* interest is the one that died." Admitting it out loud was like twisting a knife in her heart.

"Are you sure? Remember when Derek was sick a few weeks ago? Jake told me Derek was impressed by your help."

"Big deal, Dad." She grimaced. "Last Friday night Derek took Bruce MacKinnon's granddaughter out on a date."

"Bruce's granddaughter? Was she in church yesterday— that pretty girl with the red hair?"

Cheyenne nodded. "Kandi." *The girl with the cute face, perfect figure, and impressive bowling ability.* "There's no way I can compete with her."

"What do you mean?" He pulled his arm from the back of the bench. "You're every bit as pretty as that girl."

"She's tiny—just naturally thin, unlike me." Cheyenne huffed out a breath. "Derek seems crazy about her."

A minute passed before Dad spoke. "When you were a little girl, your mother would pray for you every night before we went to bed. Sometimes she prayed for a good husband for her daughter. I thought that was strange when you were so young. But Lynn was right. The years have gone by quickly, and now you're a young woman." He glanced at her, and Cheyenne was surprised to see a tear in his eye. "I'll miss you, but God will take care of you."

"Thanks, Dad." Tears crept to her own eyes, but she blinked them away. "Somehow, if I keep trusting the Lord, I know everything will work out."

Dad patted her knee. "Yep—even if you don't inherit Florence Ingersoll's money."

A sigh escaped under her breath. Why couldn't she marry the right man *and* inherit the money?

"Dad, how did you know that Mom was the one for you?

Were you super attracted to her, and you just knew she was the one?"

"No, not really. Actually I was dating another girl named Noreen. I met her at my job, and I thought *she* was the one I would marry. One Saturday our church group went ice-skating, and I invited Noreen to come along. Everything was going great until I skated into one of the girls, and she fell and broke her leg." He looked her in the eye. "That girl was your mom."

"Mom was ice-skating? I can't even picture that." Cheyenne grinned. "Are you sure *she* didn't run into *you*?"

Dad laughed. "She wasn't the most athletic person."

"Just like me." Cheyenne rolled her eyes. "So what happened? How did you and Mom get together?"

"I felt so bad for knocking her down that I volunteered to take her to the hospital. So I carried her to my car—"

"The big Wilkins body came in handy that time, huh, Dad?"

"Sure did." He grinned. "We talked all the way to the hospital, even though she was in pain. Then I hung around until her parents got there." He shook his head. "Noreen was so mad at me for leaving her."

"Well. . .you really can't blame her."

"Except for the fact that Noreen harped at me for a week. She was so jealous, and she wouldn't get off my back! Your mom was so different. The next time I saw her in church—hobbling around on crutches—she apologized for ruining my date with Noreen. Right then I realized who I wanted to marry. Your mom and I dated for three months, and I proposed to her on Valentine's Day."

Cheyenne gave a wistful sigh. "That's so romantic, Dad. I wish Mom was still here to tell me her side of the story."

"I can fill you in. Lynn had been secretly in love with me. She called it 'unrequited love.' It hurt her to see me dating Noreen."

Like me with Derek. Cheyenne sighed again, but it wasn't wistful this time.

"But Lynn bided her time and prayed a lot. Deep in her heart she knew I was destined to become her husband." He cocked an eyebrow at her. "Maybe you shouldn't give up on Derek."

"I've wanted to marry him for a long time." Why was she telling Dad this? Yet at the same time, it made her feel closer to him to share her heart. "But how do I know if he's God's will for me or if the Lord has someone else in mind?"

"Pastor Reilly says God's will is revealed through His Word. Keep studying the Bible and praying, and God will let you know. I'll pray, too. Derek's a great guy, and he'd make a wonderful husband for you." Dad glanced at his watch. "It's almost eleven. We'd better get back."

Cheyenne stood. She had a lot to pray about when she got home.

❧

Derek swung his flashlight around as he walked over the acres where the sheep had been feeding that afternoon. Shep, his collie, bounded over the hilly terrain beside him. Derek was thankful it was a warm evening, but his heart became heavier as the toll of dead bodies mounted.

Shep gave a sudden bark.

"Did you find one, boy?" Derek strode to where Shep stood, and his light passed over a small white lump. Leaning over, he trained the beam on it.

A lamb lay under the sagebrush.

He straightened. "Found another lamb, Dad," he yelled. Squatting down, he brushed his hand over the animal's tiny back. *Broken neck.* A pack of wolves must have killed all these sheep. Coyotes would have eaten what they killed, and they didn't break their necks.

Dad walked toward him, a rifle cradled in his arm. "Fourteen so far—three ewes and eleven lambs." He squinted off across the field. "We'll have to take care of the carcasses tomorrow when we can see what we're doing. Hector and Miguel will help." Dad shook his head. "Just don't know how they got past the electric fence."

Derek adjusted his cowboy hat. "We'll have to ride along the borderline tomorrow and see if there's a break. With two thousand acres of land, anything could have happened to the fence."

"That's true." Taking off his glasses, Dad rubbed his eyes. "It's almost eleven. Let's get back to the house. At least the rest of the flock are safely penned for the night."

"Yeah, too bad." Derek stood. "It's such a warm evening. I wish they could stay outside."

Falling into step, they strode together over the uneven ground back to Dad's Jeep with Shep trotting beside them. Removing his hat, Derek glanced up at the sliver of moon and the millions of stars that created a bowl above their heads. Nothing could be heard but the crunch of their footsteps until Dad spoke.

"Mom and I are thinking of turning over the ranch to you in the fall."

Derek's eyebrows shot up. "Already?"

"We saw a good deal on an RV last week, and I'm tempted to buy it. Mom wants to start traveling."

Derek slipped his hat back on. "I thought you were going to wait until you turn sixty-five."

"Why wait? That's ten years away, and Mom said she doesn't want to travel when she's decrepit." Dad laughed. "She loves traveling, and she wants to visit the states she's never seen, especially in the South." He looked at Derek as they strode side by side. "You'll have the house to yourself, son. Might as well get married and have a passel of kids. Maybe you'll end up marrying that MacKinnon girl you took out to dinner last Friday."

Derek shook his head. "Not Kandi." He turned to his dad. "To be honest, I'm confused. Every time I pray about my future, it seems that God is telling me to stay single in order to serve Him. But I'd like to get married someday." Cheyenne's pretty blue eyes entered his thoughts. "I'm just not sure what God's will is right now."

Approaching the Jeep, they both climbed in, and Shep jumped into the back. Dad started the engine.

A cool night breeze hit the brim of Derek's hat, and he removed it. "Dad, how did you know Mom was the right one for you? Did the Lord strike you with a lightning bolt, and you just knew she was the one?"

"No, that's not what happened at all." Dad shifted gears, and the Jeep rolled over the uneven ground. "Your mom was the prettiest girl in high school, but she was dating my best friend, Kyle. The three of us hung out together, and the more I got to know your mom, the more I liked her. She was a lot of fun." He paused. "Then during our senior year, I realized I was falling in love. I wanted to spend the rest of my life with her."

Derek grinned. "So you stole her right under Kyle's nose, and she willingly ran into your arms."

"I wish. Unfortunately I didn't have the gumption to do that. But Kyle was always starting arguments with Yvette, and I would get so mad at him for yelling at her." Dad looked at him. "She would yell right back."

"Yep, that's Mom."

Dad stared out the windshield as they slowly bumped along. "Somehow I always managed to calm them down, and they would get back together time after time."

"You missed your calling, Dad. You should have been a marriage counselor."

"Ha! I'm more suited for sheep. They don't argue with you."

"That's why I like sheep." Derek grinned. "So how did you and Mom finally start dating?"

"She and Kyle had another fight, a real humdinger. When I confronted Kyle, he asked me to talk to Yvette for him. To plead his case, so to speak."

"Sounds like *The Courtship of Miles Standish*."

Dad glanced at him. "That's exactly what happened! I took

your mom to this little diner that evening and told her Kyle wanted to get back with her." A half smile shadowed his face. "She laid her hand on my arm and said, 'Jake, I'm tired of fighting with Kyle. I want someone who's more easygoing— like you.' I was stunned!"

"That was a bold move on Mom's part."

"Later she told me she had wanted to date me for months. She tried to break up with Kyle, but he wouldn't let go. When I took her to the diner, she knew this was her one and only opportunity to let me know how she felt."

Derek nodded. "She seemed to know what the Lord had for her. But how am I supposed to know God's will?"

"Keep it in prayer, son. God will make the way clear." Dad parked the Jeep in back of the house and opened the driver's door.

Derek climbed out of the passenger's side. He had a lot to pray about.

eight

Cheyenne smiled at the elderly woman on the other side of the post office counter. "Here's your change, Mrs. Hochstetler." She dropped a few coins into the outstretched hand.

"Thank you, dear." The thin lips curved into a smile, revealing straight dentures. Mrs. Hochstetler slowly turned, and the bell over the door jangled as she walked outside.

Glancing out into the customer area, Cheyenne noticed some crooked mailing boxes in the display. She walked around the counter, and the bell over the door rang again. A tall, middle-aged woman dressed in a yellow pantsuit walked in. Her short brown hair was smoothly styled, and Cheyenne gazed at her pretty face, thinking she looked familiar.

The woman stopped and put her hands on her hips. "Why, Cheyenne Wilkins!"

Cheyenne gasped. "Mrs. Oliver!" She reached out to give the woman a hug. "I almost didn't recognize you with that different hairstyle." Janet Oliver and her husband had been members of their church since Cheyenne was a little girl, and Janet had been a close friend with Cheyenne's mom. But the couple moved away several years ago.

Janet hugged her then gripped Cheyenne's forearms so she could look at her. "It is awesome to see you again! You look absolutely wonderful." She shook her head. "I can see your mother in your face. You look just like her, and she was such a beautiful woman."

"Thanks." Cheyenne smiled. "It's great to see you again, Mrs. Oliver."

The bell jingled, and they both turned in time to see Agatha Collingsworth walk in.

"Why, Aggie!" Janet left Cheyenne to give her a hug. "Don't you look good!"

"Oh my word!" Aggie hugged her back. "Janet Oliver! It's been so long."

Janet stood back. "It's only been four years since we moved away. You're still doing business at The Beauty Spot, I presume?"

Aggie nodded. "Yep, still at it. Why are you in town, Janet?"

"I'm moving back to Fort Lob." Her light-brown eyes flitted over to Cheyenne, and she touched her arm. "Remember when you took piano lessons from me? Do you still play the piano?"

"Never." Cheyenne laughed. "We still have the piano at our house, but no one has touched it for years."

"That's a shame." Janet's thin eyebrows dipped into a frown. "I'll have to come by and tickle those ivories."

Aggie perused Janet's hairstyle. "Why are you moving back?"

"You probably heard that Fred died last year. My cousin, Adelaide, lives in Fort Lob, and we only have each other now. No one else in the whole world. So I thought I might as well move back."

"Adelaide is your only relative?" Cheyenne couldn't imagine that.

"The only one. Fred and I never had any children, and Adelaide's husband and son died years ago."

"I'm sorry to hear that."

Janet's voice softened. "Thank you, dear."

She turned back to talk to Aggie, and Cheyenne studied the woman. She was almost as tall as Cheyenne, but she certainly had a better figure. *I am going to firm up this flab!* Maybe a new wardrobe would be good, too.

If Janet Oliver could look like a million bucks, so could she.

&

Cheyenne glanced at the clock. *Almost five.* Janet and Aggie had stayed for an hour, but fortunately the post office had not had any customers while they were shooting the breeze.

And we probably won't have any more. She entered the back room and took the door key from the hook on the wall. *Might as well lock up for the day.*

The bell rang as the door opened.

Then again, maybe not.

She walked out from the back room. Carrying a medium-sized Priority mailing box, Derek Brandt approached the counter.

His eyes met hers, and her pulse quickened.

"Hi, Cheyenne." He set the box on the counter. "Mom wants to mail this box to Grandma in Casper." He pulled his wallet from his back pocket.

"Do you need any insurance or delivery confirmation?" She lifted the box to the scale.

"Nah, just send it."

She glanced at the readout. "That will be four dollars and eighty-three cents."

Derek handed her a five-dollar bill. "Glad I made it to the post office. Wasn't sure if you would still be open."

She dropped the change in his hand. "I was just about to lock up when you—"

The bell jangled again. Cheyenne glanced at the door, and Derek turned his head. Rex Pierson walked inside. Cheyenne frowned. He had already come in this morning to check his post office box and stayed to talk to her between customers.

"Hey, neighbor!" Derek stuck out his hand as Rex strode to the counter.

Rex shook it. "Howdy, Brandt," he drawled. "Good to see you."

Cheyenne eyed the two men. They were the same height, so Rex must be six three, although Rex was thinner than Derek. And he looked a lot older. She listened as they talked for five minutes about a cattle auction next week. Finally she moved to the door, key in hand, and waited.

Derek glanced at her. "Guess it's time to leave, Rex." He winked at her as he walked to the door. "I think Cheyenne is giving us a subtle hint."

Her heart fluttered at his wink. "Well. . .it is past five o'clock."

Rex stepped toward the wall of post office boxes. "I need to check on my mail. See you around, Brandt." He thrust a key in one of the boxes.

"Later, Rex." Derek moved past Cheyenne as he exited. "Bye, Cheyenne." He didn't look back as he walked outside.

A cloud of disappointment hung over her as she turned and waited for Rex. Derek wasn't paying her much attention. He must be serious about Kandi MacKinnon. Or maybe he was going back to his no-marriage-until-forty policy.

Well, no matter. She would move to Loveland and find someone else.

"No more mail." Rex closed his box and turned the key.

Cheyenne grinned. "I could have told you that. Bernie and I fill the post office boxes every morning before we open. Once you get your mail for the day, that's it. No more until tomorrow."

Rex turned to her, and that slow smile curved his lips. "I knew that. Just waiting for Brandt to leave." He frowned. "What's his first name?"

"Derek." Cheyenne bit her lower lip. Why was Rex hanging around?

"Oh yeah—Derek. And his dad's name?"

"Jake."

Rex nodded. "Derek and Jake. Good family. Mrs. Brandt made me a pie when I first moved in. Apple."

Cheyenne smiled. "That was nice of her."

"Yeah. I'm not much of a baker, so it was appreciated." Rex cleared his throat. "Uh, Cheyenne, I was wondering. . .uh, if you'd like to go to supper with me tonight."

Her lips parted. *He's asking me out?*

She met his brown eyes and saw uncertainty there. It made her heart melt. She'd heard through the grapevine that Rex was a widower, and he must be lonely. "I'd love to eat with you."

He visibly relaxed. "Great! Um, the Cattlemen's Diner?"

The pros and cons of that eating establishment sprinted through her mind. It was close—a walk across the street—so she wouldn't have to ride with him to a restaurant, but their dining experience would fuel local gossip. Certain people in Fort Lob would have her married to Rex Pierson by sunset.

But who cared what other people thought? She and Rex were just friends.

"The Cattlemen's Diner is fine." She turned and locked the door. "You can go out the back way with me."

Together they walked outside and crossed the street. Rex held the door for her as they entered the restaurant. Within ten minutes they were seated across from each other in a booth by the front window, and Sara Stine, a high school senior, took their orders. Rex requested a steak with mashed potatoes. Cheyenne ordered fish with rice pilaf.

As Sara left, Cheyenne glanced around the busy restaurant. "I haven't been to the Cattlemen's Diner for years, but not much has changed." In the corner, the jukebox crooned an oldie, and the sounds of clashing silverware and loud conversation filled the room.

Rex's brown eyes met hers. "I'm starting to recognize a few faces. Seems like the same people eat in here every night."

Cheyenne raised her eyebrows. "You eat here every evening?"

He nodded. "So far."

Opening her mouth, she was about to issue him an invitation to eat at her house tomorrow night. But the way his eyes stared at her clamped her lips shut. For more than a week, he had talked to her every day at the post office, and now he had asked her out.

Most likely, Rex Pierson's end goal was matrimony.

Cheyenne's stomach clenched. She studied his tan, weathered face with new eyes, remembering that she had asked the Lord to send her a man. If she was going to inherit Grandmother's fortune, she needed to get married—and soon.

Was Rex the one?

Obviously Derek was not interested in a relationship with her, especially with Kandi MacKinnon hanging around.

But did Cheyenne want to marry this old rancher?

I don't have to decide that tonight. She would be a good friend to Rex—and see where their relationship led.

She took a deep breath. "Why did you move to Wyoming, Rex?"

"Always wanted to own a ranch." He steepled his work-worn, knobby fingers in front of his face. "For years I worked for my brother on his ranch 'cause my wife wanted to live in town." His eyes darted around the restaurant before reconnecting with hers. "When she passed on a couple years ago, I thought I'd see what ranches were for sale." He shrugged. "Looked at ranches in four different states, finally settlin' on the one here."

With a smile, she nodded. "The old Dudley place. My mom and I visited Mr. and Mrs. Dudley several times when I was a girl. The house is quite small, as I remember."

Folding his arms on the table, he leaned forward. "Just a little one-floor bungalow. I'd like to expand it after I get married. Might even have some kids someday. That's why I'm looking to marry a younger woman. A good Christian woman."

His eyes held hers, and his left eyebrow hiked up slightly, as if asking what she thought about that.

Cheyenne drew in a quick breath. Forget the local gossip! In Rex's mind, they were already destined for the altar.

❧

"This is our house right here." Cheyenne pointed to the right, and Rex pulled his rattling truck into the driveway.

He glanced at the house. "Looks dark, except for the porch light."

"Dad left that on for me. He's probably in bed."

It was Saturday night, and Rex had taken her to a movie in Lusk. Now it was after midnight, and Cheyenne felt a twinge of nerves clench her stomach. Would Rex kiss her good night?

Did she want him to?

On Thursday evening, after they'd eaten at the Cattlemen's Diner, he had walked her back across the street to the post office parking lot, opened her car door for her, and wished her a pleasant evening. She thanked him for the dinner and drove away. But now. . .

Rex shifted the gears into PARK and switched off the key. With a shudder, the engine gave up the ghost. "I'll get your door." He exited the truck and walked around it.

As she waited, her mind replayed the evening. She could barely recall what the movie was about after Rex put his arm around her in the darkened theater. With slight pressure from his fingers, she moved closer to him until her head rested on his shoulder. After the movie, they got ice cream at the local Dairy Queen, sitting across from each other at a tiny two-person table. Rex leaned in as they ate, his eyes gazing into hers, his attention never waning. She gazed back, but nothing stirred inside her.

The truck door creaked open. "Let me help you down, Cheyenne."

"Thanks." She took his rough hand to climb out of the cab, and a soft breeze lifted her hair. "It's a warm night."

"Sure thing." Rex didn't let go, and they walked hand in hand toward the house.

Cheyenne felt the need to keep talking. "This is late for you, isn't it? I'm sure you get up early every morning to take care of your animals."

"Yeah." His calloused fingers squeezed hers. "But I don't need much sleep. Four or five hours will do me."

"Really?" They crossed the porch to the front door. "I need at least seven."

Rex dropped her hand and faced her. "Guess I'd better let you go then." He smiled, and his eyes gleamed in the porch light.

Cheyenne's stomach clenched a little tighter, and she took a small step back. "Thanks so much for taking me out, Rex.

I had a nice time."

"Me, too." He opened his arms. "Let me hug you 'fore I go."

A hug. Okay, she could handle that.

Stepping into his embrace, she draped her arms around his thin frame. It wasn't like hugging her dad, who was hefty, but Rex was closer to her dad's age than he was to hers. Dad had just turned fifty-two. How old was Rex? Was he old enough to be her father?

After a prolonged squeeze, he stepped back. " 'Night, Cheyenne."

"Good night."

Opening the door of the house, she stepped inside and softly closed the door behind her. In the dark she waited until she heard Rex's truck wheeze to life. He revved the engine a couple times, and she could just imagine how those fumes permeated the air. Then the gears shifted, and the vehicle rattled down the road, the sound becoming fainter until it was gone.

Cheyenne closed her eyes and leaned against the door. *Lord, is Rex really the man You sent me?*

With a sigh, she walked through the darkened living room and sank down to the sofa, not bothering to turn on the light. Her attraction to Rex Pierson was just as dark as the room. When he gazed into her eyes, there was no electric spark, no tingle, no jolt of awareness.

Nothing like the chemistry she had with Derek.

Why don't I have any passion for Rex, Lord? Certainly the God who made her could change her desires so she would swoon in Rex Pierson's presence.

But maybe this would be a different kind of romantic relationship—the kind where love sneaks in silently, after years of marriage, and one day she would wake up to discover that she loved her husband.

With a groan, she laid her head back on the sofa. "I don't want that kind of marriage, Lord!" She had felt more passion for some of the boys she dated in college, even the ones she knew she would never marry.

Enough of this! Standing, she walked to her bedroom. She passed Dad's bedroom and heard soft snoring. At least she hadn't awoken him.

Closing her bedroom door, she flipped on the light switch, blinking in the brightness. Then she dropped to her knees beside her bed.

"Heavenly Father, all I can do is put this relationship in Your hands. I don't know if Rex is the one for me or not, but he's a good Christian man, and I'm willing to give him a chance."

She still wanted Grandmother's millions, but money was a poor substitute for love. The important thing was to marry the right man.

As soon as possible.

nine

On Sunday morning, Derek walked into the church auditorium after his Sunday school class. He couldn't believe it was the third week of July already. It seemed the summer had just started, and now it was half finished.

Time flies when you're getting old.

As he ambled down the center aisle toward his usual spot, he glanced ahead and saw Cheyenne sitting with Rex Pierson in the third row. Rex had his arm draped on the pew behind her.

Derek stopped. *What in the world?*

Kandi MacKinnon stepped in front of him. "Hi, Derek." She smiled.

It took him a moment to focus on her. "Oh hi, Kandi. We missed you in the Single Servings this morning. I'm glad you made it to church."

She moved closer. "Grandpa wasn't feeling well this morning so he decided to skip Sunday school. But after a while he felt better, and we decided to come. Can you sit with us?"

Amazing—three sentences! "Uh. . ." He hesitated as musical laughter reached his ears, and he glanced toward Cheyenne. She was looking at Rex, an angelic smile on her pretty face. If he sat in his usual spot, he would be sitting right behind them. He turned to Kandi. "Sure, I'll sit with you." He followed her to a pew down front on the right—the opposite side from where Cheyenne and Rex were sitting.

Bruce MacKinnon stood to let them slide into the pew. He shook hands with Derek then sat down beside him.

Kandi smiled up at him. "I haven't seen you since last Sunday. What have you been doing all week?"

"Just working on the ranch." He leaned back in the pew.

"Dad and I had to fix the fence. It took us two days to find the spot where wolves broke in. They killed fourteen sheep last Monday."

Her eyes widened. "Oh?"

"It was just senseless killing." He grit his teeth. "It still wrenches my heart out to think about those wolves killing poor defenseless ewes and lambs."

Frowning, she looked down. "Oh."

She must be all talked out. Derek turned to Bruce. "I hear you're not feeling well."

"It's just my arthritis. Some days are—"

"Why, Bruce MacKinnon!"

The female voice caused both men to look up. A tall woman in a light-blue suit, whom Derek recognized as Janet Oliver, stood beside the pew and beamed down at Bruce.

"Well, my goodness!" Bruce jumped up and pumped her hand. He didn't seem to have any trouble with his arthritis now. "So good to see you, Janet. Welcome back to Fort Lob."

She laughed. "Thank you, Bruce. I feel like I've come home."

Kandi leaned toward Derek. "Who's that?"

"Janet Oliver—my sister's piano teacher. She and her husband moved away a few years ago."

"Oh." Kandi gazed at her grandfather and Janet as they continued their animated conversation.

Derek lowered his voice. "She has an outgoing personality, as you can see, and she was always quite a showman on the piano."

He turned back to watch, and Janet caught his eye. She leaned into the pew. "Now you look familiar."

He stood and held out his hand. "Derek Brandt, Mrs. Oliver."

"Derek!" Her mouth dropped as she squeezed his hand. "I can't believe how tall you are! And how old are you now? Twenty-three? Twenty-four?"

"Twenty-six." He didn't glance around, but the auditorium

was quiet. He figured the entire congregation must be witnessing this exchange.

"No!" Janet gave his hand a shake before she dropped it. "Why Derek, you make me feel so old!"

He grinned, not sure how to answer that declaration. Fortunately he was saved by Aggie, who made a sudden appearance. The two women gabbed a minute before Aggie invited Janet to sit with them. They got settled in the pew as Wayne Holland, the song director, announced the first hymn. The congregation stood.

Sharing a hymnbook with Kandi, Derek sang out on "Amazing Grace." Beside him Janet belted out the words, almost covering Aggie's southern twang. Derek couldn't hear Kandi's voice at all, although she seemed to be singing. Must be because he was way up here in the stratosphere and she was a foot lower. He glanced down on her red hair. It shone in the overhead lights, looking soft. But it didn't make his heart beat any faster.

He glanced across the auditorium at Cheyenne. Singing, she smiled as she stood next to Rex. *What does she see in him?* Rex Pierson was nothing but an old wizened cowhand. He looked about fifty.

Derek sat down with the rest of the congregation as Pastor Reilly stepped to the pulpit.

"We have an unusual announcement this morning." The pastor's aged gray eyes squinted as he gazed over the auditorium. "A Christian organization is hosting a trip to Yellowstone National Park. They have asked several churches, including ours, for volunteer counselors to accompany elementary-age children."

Derek raised his eyebrows. *I would love to do that!*

"The dates are Friday, August 7, through Sunday, August 9." The pastor motioned toward the left side of the auditorium. "Ralph Little is taking down the names of the volunteers, so please see him after the service if you're interested."

Derek made a mental note to talk to Ralph. This was exactly the way he wanted to spend his life—serving the Lord through mission trips. He still had his eye on that trip to Honduras, where a missionary needed help building his church. So how could Derek get married? His wife would want him to stay home all the time.

Unless she had a servant's heart and accompanied him.

He glanced at Cheyenne. Rex had his arm around her, and a prick of jealousy hit Derek. Why had he always thought of her as nothing more than a good friend—the girl his sisters hung out with? She was a beautiful woman, but it looked like she had found someone else.

Cheyenne is out. He glanced down at the girl beside him. *Kandi is definitely out.*

But why was he even thinking about a relationship? His original idea to get married after he turned forty was looking better all the time.

❧

As the church service ended, Cheyenne turned to Rex. "I'm going to sign up for the Yellowstone outing." Her heart gave a little leap.

"Okay, whatever." Rex glanced at his watch. "I need to get back to the ranch and check on Bessie. If she don't start rallying, I'll have to call the vet." He looked at Cheyenne. "How about you sign up for the Yellowstone thing, I'll go check on Bessie, and then I'll pick you up at your house, and we'll go out for lunch."

She smiled. "Okay. Let's do that."

Rex smiled back—that slow smile that made him look handsome. "I'm taking you to a steak and potatoes restaurant I found in Douglas."

"Mindy's Diner?"

With a little grunt, he folded his arms. "You already know the place?"

Cheyenne laughed. "I've lived in this area all my life, Rex. I know every restaurant within a two-hundred-mile radius."

He chuckled. "If you say so, pretty lady. Pick you up in an hour, okay?"

"Sure."

He winked at her before walking down the aisle toward the church door. Cheyenne watched him, and a small sigh escaped. That wink should have raised her heartbeat or her blood pressure—something!

Ralph Little stood at the back of the auditorium, and she made her way toward him. "Ralph, I'd like to sign up for that Yellowstone outing."

"Thanks for volunteering." He handed her a clipboard and a pen. "Just fill out this information."

Cheyenne glanced down the page-long application. "What organization is hosting this?"

"The Bolton Creek Children's Home near Casper. It's run by Mr. and Mrs. Frank Lindley." Ralph raised his thin gray eyebrows. "Ever hear of them?"

She shook her head. "Can't say that I have."

"The Lindleys have been the houseparents there for thirty years. They've seen hundreds of kids go through their place. Right now they have eighteen orphans."

Hmm. . .an orphanage.

Ralph motioned to her application. "This is a field trip for the children. Frank told me they wanted to give the staff a weekend off."

What would it be like to work in an orphanage? She had never thought of that before.

By the time she finished filling out the form, most of the congregation had left, except for Bruce and Aggie who were conversing with Janet Oliver. Derek stood nearby talking to Kandi. The girl gazed up at him, her green eyes shining as she listened. Cheyenne's heart took a dive.

She clenched her teeth. *Why am I still pining after him?* Old habits die hard, and she needed to kill this one. Rex was part of her life now. So what if she wasn't super attracted to him? He was a great guy, and she could learn to love him.

Couldn't she?

She turned to Ralph and handed him the clipboard. "Here you go."

"Thanks." He tucked it into a soft-sided black leather case. "Looks like you might be the only volunteer from our church."

Cheyenne raised her eyebrows. "But this is such a great opportunity. I'm surprised no one else—"

"Ralph, wait!"

Cheyenne turned at Derek's voice.

"I want to sign up for Yellowstone." Derek's glance cut to Cheyenne. "You going, too?"

She nodded. "It sounds like fun."

"It does, doesn't it?"

Ralph thrust a clipboard under Derek's nose. "Here's an application, Derek."

"Okay." Derek took the clipboard and glanced at the paper. "Who's sponsoring this trip?"

"The Bolton Creek Children's Home." Ralph raised his eyebrows at Derek. "Have you ever heard of them?"

"The orphanage in Casper?" Derek smiled. "I've known the Lindleys for years."

Kandi stepped toward Ralph. "I'd like to sign up, too."

"Certainly!" He pulled another clipboard from his briefcase and handed it to her.

Cheyenne bit her lower lip. Kandi didn't seem like the outdoor type. She must be following Derek to Yellowstone. Or maybe he talked her into going with him.

Taking a step back, Cheyenne gave a little wave. "Thanks, Ralph. See you all later."

Derek glanced up. "See you around, Cheyenne."

For a brief second, their eyes locked before he looked back down, and her heart tripped at his piercing gaze. She turned away, her thoughts in turmoil. *Why does he still affect me like that and Rex doesn't affect me at all?* Obviously Derek was falling in love with Kandi. And Cheyenne had Rex.

No, Rex has me.

As much as she hated to admit it, her heart still belonged to Derek Brandt. Maybe she should stick to her original plan and move to Loveland.

❧

Derek pulled his truck out of the church parking lot. He glanced across the bench seat and gave Kandi a tight smile. She had asked him to take her to the Cattlemen's Diner for lunch since Bruce and Aggie had invited Jim Wilkins and Janet Oliver out to eat, and the four of them planned to catch up on old times.

Kandi could have gone with them.

Ah, well. . .Christian charity. He had to eat somewhere since Mom and Dad were in Denver visiting Ryan and his family, and he might as well have someone to eat with, even if his dinner partner was almost mute.

At the end of Bighorn Avenue, he braked at the STOP sign and glanced to his left. Cheyenne stood on the corner, waiting to cross Main Street.

Derek rolled down his window. "Hey, Cheyenne! Need a lift?"

She looked up at him before smiling. "That would be great!" She stepped off the curb to walk around the front of the truck.

Derek nodded to Kandi as he rolled up his window. "Move over."

She slid over to the middle. "Is Cheyenne coming to the restaurant with us?"

He hesitated. *That would be awkward.* "No, I'll just give her a ride home."

Kandi frowned. "Why? She can walk."

"Christian charity," he whispered.

Cheyenne climbed into the cab and sat down. "Thanks for the ride, Derek." She closed the door then turned to him with a smile. "Rex wanted to check on a sick cow before we go out to lunch. He told me to wait for him at home."

Rex. She was really falling for that guy. "But where's your car?" Derek turned right on Main Street.

Cheyenne sighed. "The old Dart finally bit the dust."

"So it's at Tom's shop?"

"No, Dad wants me to junk it."

"Really?" Raising his eyebrows, he glanced at her.

She nodded. "Dad wants me to buy a good used car at Skinny's."

Kandi turned to Cheyenne with a frown. "Skinny's?"

Derek laughed. "Skinny Olander. The slickest car salesman in the West."

Cheyenne nodded. "Did you know that Dad grew up with Skinny? They attended the same high school in Bismarck."

"No joke?" Derek grinned. "Was he always trying to pawn something off on other students? Maybe a good piece of swampland in Florida?"

She laughed. "Probably. Dad has bought all his cars from Skinny." She fell silent a moment as Derek rounded the corner of her street. "I wanted to go there tomorrow since it's my day off, but Dad has to mind the store. Both Harold and Dale are taking vacation this week."

"I'll take you." The words were out of Derek's mouth before he thought. But why shouldn't he drive her to Douglas tomorrow? His dad would be back from Denver tonight, which would free up Derek at the ranch.

"That's all right, Derek. Dad and I can go next Monday."

He pulled the truck into her driveway. "I don't mind, Cheyenne. Besides, I want to look at the kind of cars he's selling now. I haven't been to Skinny's in years." He paused. "I'll pick you up tomorrow morning, say, nine o'clock?"

"Okay. Thanks." She opened the door and climbed down. "And thanks for the lift."

"You're welcome." He smiled as she closed the door and walked to the house. Shifting gears, he backed out the driveway.

Kandi stayed in the middle next to him. "I suppose that's Christian charity, too?"

Derek glanced at her. "What? Taking Cheyenne to Douglas tomorrow?"

She nodded.

"I suppose it is." He shrugged. "She needs a ride, and I can take the day off. Why shouldn't I volunteer to help her out?"

Kandi said nothing, and Derek bit back a sigh.

Their lunch was going to be very short.

ten

"Cheyenne, have you been to Yellowstone before?"

"Once, when I was little." She looked at Derek as he drove her to Douglas the next morning. Under her breath, she gave a wistful sigh. He was so handsome. Too bad he was dating Kandi.

Of course, she was dating Rex. She thought about their lunch yesterday. It was. . .nice, but not thrilling. And he had yet to kiss her. Maybe once he kissed her, she would feel like they were a real couple. Maybe she would start falling in love with him.

"You've only gone once?" Derek's dark-blue eyes met hers. "Yellowstone is so close, Cheyenne."

She shrugged. "It must be true what they say about having a tourist place in your backyard. You never visit it."

"That's not true for me. I've been to Yellowstone so many times I've lost count. And I love mountain climbing. I'm glad we have the Rockies in our backyard."

She shook her head. "You're so athletic. If I went mountain climbing, I'd end up in the hospital."

"How about skiing?" He glanced at her before looking back at the road. "I bet you went skiing last winter. Maybe in Vail or Aspen?"

Her eyes widened. "Me? Miss Klutz? You've got to be kidding!"

He grinned. "Okay, no skiing. But wouldn't you like to try it?" He waggled his eyebrows.

Cheyenne's defenses weakened considerably. Derek was just too handsome, and he was so easy to talk to. "You don't understand. Walking Dad's dog on the sidewalk is almost beyond me. How would I ever be able to ski down a mountain?"

"It's fun. I could teach you."

"Oh sure." She pictured herself trying to ski—and falling. Of course, if she fell into Derek's arms, that wouldn't be such a bad thing.

"Here we are." He pulled into the parking lot full of new cars. The sign read SKINNY'S QUALITY NEW AND PRE-OWNED VEHICLES. "Looks like a quality place."

Cheyenne glanced at all the triangle flags that decorated the lot, and her stomach cramped. "I hope he has a good used car for me. Dad called him on Saturday and told him my price range."

"Since Skinny knows you, I'm sure he'll give you a good deal."

She cocked an eyebrow at Derek. "Actually, I've never met the guy. I bought my Dart from Horace Frankenberg."

Five minutes later, she stepped into the showroom. Derek walked in behind her.

"Welcome to Skinny's Vehicles!" A rotund man dressed in a tight-fitting brown suit approached her. Tufts of gray hair surrounded his bald head. He stuck out a large hand. "I'm Skinny. And you're Jim Wilkins's daughter, right?" Barely waiting for a nod from Cheyenne, he continued. "You look just like your mother—an extremely beautiful woman."

Hmm. . .a flattering car salesman. Cheyenne smiled as she shook his hand. "I'm Cheyenne Wilkins."

He raised bushy eyebrows. "Cheyenne? Like the city? Wow, that name fits you! Beautiful name!"

Derek coughed and turned toward the nearest car model. He studied the sticker price in the window.

Cheyenne wanted to poke Derek in the ribs. She smiled at the salesman. "My dad asked you to show me a good used car."

"Right. I have so many good vehicles that I picked out a couple to show you." Skinny held the outer door open for her and followed her outside.

As they walked down a row of cars, Cheyenne noticed that

Derek had come outside, too. She motioned to him. "Derek, come over here."

He joined them, and Skinny thrust out his hand. "You must be the significant other."

Derek shook his hand, not correcting Skinny's impression. "Derek Brandt."

"Glad to meet you! Now." Skinny turned to a dark-green car. "Here we have a 1997 Saturn. Runs like a top." He opened the driver's door. "Sit down here, Cheyenne. I'll show you the controls."

She took a seat, and he pointed things out on the instrument panel.

Skinny straightened. "Would you like to take this one for a spin?"

Derek opened the passenger door and leaned inside. "You don't want this one, Cheyenne. There's hail damage on the roof."

"Really?" Cheyenne stood and looked at the roof. Sure enough, the entire thing was pockmarked. "Skinny, can I look at another car?"

"Hey, I'll subtract a hundred dollars for the damage."

Cheyenne glanced at Derek. With a frown, he gave a slight shake of his head. She turned to the car salesman. "I think I'd rather look at another one."

"Okay." He gave Derek a dark look. "Let's walk down here."

She followed him to a wine-colored car, and Derek walked by her side.

"You'll like this one, Cheyenne." Skinny placed his hand on the roof. "Wonderful car! A 2003 Cavalier with low mileage." He tapped the sticker price in the back window. "It's a little higher than your dad wanted to pay, but a real steal at this price."

Derek looked at the sticker before walking around the car.

Skinny opened the driver's door. "Take a seat, Cheyenne. We'll take this one for a spin."

Within five minutes, they were on the road. Skinny sat in the passenger seat, talking the entire time. Derek sat in the back. After riding around the streets of Douglas, she drove the car back on the lot.

"Nice, huh?" Skinny smiled at her. "Let's go inside, and we can fill out the paperwork."

Cheyenne got out and whispered to Derek. "What do you think?"

"Looks like a good car." He raised his eyebrows. "Do you want it?"

She studied the sticker price. "I like it, but it's so much money—about a thousand more than I can afford."

Derek turned to Skinny. "Take off a thousand dollars, and she'll take it."

"A thousand?" Skinny shook his head. "Five hundred is all I can afford to subtract on this beauty. It's such a good car. A real steal at this price already."

Derek turned to Cheyenne. "I saw a couple other used car places when we were—"

"Okay!" Skinny turned to the office. "A thousand off. Let's do the paperwork."

Cheyenne smiled at Derek as they walked together. "Thanks, Derek. I couldn't have done this without you."

"Hey, that's what friends are for." Placing his arm around her shoulders, he gave her a squeeze.

She looked up at him. For an instant their gazes held, and then he opened the door for her.

Cheyenne walked inside, her heart thumping.

Would she ever have that kind of chemistry with Rex?

❧

On Thursday afternoon, Derek walked into the mudroom and pulled off his boots. The good smell of fried chicken wafted out from the kitchen. His stomach growled, and he glanced at his watch. Mom would have supper ready in twenty minutes, and that would give him just enough time to take a shower.

Wiping his shirtsleeve across his forehead, he entered the kitchen. His mom and Tonya sat at the table talking. They both turned to him.

"Oh good, you're here." Mom stood and lifted a pan lid on the stove. "Is Dad coming?"

"Yeah, he was cleaning up." Derek raised his eyebrows at Tonya. "Hey, sis. What are you doing here?"

"Murray is working a two-day shift, so Mom invited me over for supper." She glanced at his dirty jeans. "Hard day with the sheep?"

He shrugged. "Normal day. I spent all afternoon checking for cuts and cleaning them." He walked to the dining room door, ready to go upstairs.

"Derek, guess what?"

He turned back.

Tonya's dark eyes took on a sudden shine. "This morning I signed the contract to get my cookbook published!"

"Wow, congratulations!" She had been working on writing her own cookbook for years. "So when are we going to see the published book?"

"It won't come out until next year. But this never would have happened if Lane Hutchins wasn't my brother-in-law. He got me in with his agent."

Mom laid her hand on Tonya's shoulder. "You don't know that, honey. You might have been published without Lane's help. God works in mysterious ways."

"Maybe." Tonya gave a happy sigh. "I'm just glad the Lord let it happen."

Derek grinned. "Another published author in the family. Congrats again, sis." Turning, he ambled through the dining room. As he entered the living room, he heard Tonya ask Mom about their new neighbor.

"His name is Rex Pierson," Mom said. "He's dating Cheyenne."

Derek stopped beside the piano and glanced back the way he had come.

"Yeah, I noticed them sitting together at church." Tonya's voice sounded far away, but Derek could hear her clearly. "What do you know about him?"

"Dad and I went over to his ranch last week." The sounds of a drawer opening and silverware clinking competed with Mom's voice. "That place has been vacant for so long, it was a mess. But Rex is a hard worker."

"Is he raising sheep?"

"Cattle. He brought eight cows with him from Montana then went to auction yesterday and bought ninety-two head. So now he'll have an even hundred. They're supposed to be delivered on Friday."

Derek already knew all that, so he continued to the stairway. He shouldn't be eavesdropping anyway. But as he stepped on the first stair, Tonya's voice stopped him.

"I heard that Rex is in the market for a wife. Gloria Schutzenhofer says he has his sights set on Cheyenne."

"Well, she deserves a good husband." Mom's voice softened, and Derek crept back to the dining room. "We had always hoped she'd end up as Derek's wife, but I guess that wasn't to be."

"That's what Callie and I were hoping." Tonya sighed. "Don't know what's wrong with that guy."

A chair scraped on the kitchen tile. "Derek thinks the Lord wants him to remain single so he can serve Him."

"What? That's crazy. He doesn't have to remain single to serve the Lord."

"I know, but that's what he wants to do." Mom sighed. "Did Gloria have anything else to say about Rex?"

"He and his wife were married for eighteen years, but they didn't have any children." Tonya paused. "I guess she was a sickly woman, and Rex took care of her. She died two years ago."

"That's sad. I hope he gets a good wife."

Derek walked to the stairway, not waiting for Tonya's reply. *Cheyenne would make a fantastic wife.*

He thought of the sparks of electricity that often arced

between them. Did she have that kind of chemistry with Rex? Did he appreciate her? Her beauty, her friendliness, her kindness?

A frown pulled at his mouth as he climbed the stairs. *I should steal her away from that guy.*

Startled by the thought, he stopped. His mind drifted back to the conversation he'd had with his dad last week.

"So you stole her right under Kyle's nose, and she willingly ran into your arms."

"I wish. Unfortunately I didn't have the gumption to do that."

Derek continued on his way upstairs.

Gumption.

Did he have the nerve, the courage to win Cheyenne? Or was he just jealous?

Lord, what is Your will? Maybe the good Lord brought Rex Pierson to Wyoming just to marry Cheyenne Wilkins. And maybe Derek would remain single for life.

Is that what I really want?

Reaching the top of the stairs, he said a silent prayer. He was more confused than ever.

eleven

Early on the last Monday of July, Cheyenne drove her car under The Rocking B Ranch archway and down the long driveway to the Brandt home. Callie had invited her to join their family for the pancake breakfast at Cheyenne Frontier Days and spend the rest of the day at the rodeo.

Last year Cheyenne had gone with the Brandt family, spending the entire day hanging around with Derek. She looked back on that day with fond memories, but it hadn't changed their relationship much.

This year she thought she would go to Frontier Days with Rex, but he was busy getting his ranch settled. The cattle he bought at auction had arrived, plus he was interviewing several men today for "hired hand" positions.

Five dates. That was the extent of their relationship, plus sitting beside him in church, and Rex had yet to kiss her good night. But he always hugged her, and she enjoyed talking to him, getting to know him. He entered her thoughts more often, and she was beginning to view him as her future husband. If they could get married by the end of this year and have a child next year, that would take care of Grandmother's will.

She gave a little shiver. When her thirtieth birthday rolled around, she would be a millionaire—with her husband and child. The thought made her head spin.

But today Cheyenne would forget about Grandmother's will. She would relax and enjoy some "girl time" with Callie.

Exiting the car, she took a deep breath of warm Wyoming air. A few birds twittered in the large oak tree by the two-story farmhouse. Besides that, the place was quiet. Peaceful. She looked up at the expansive sky, still streaked with pink and orange from the sunrise. Cheyenne gazed at the rolling hills spreading to the east as far as her eye could see. Rex's ranch was over there somewhere. Someday, hopefully soon, she would live on that ranch, and the Brandts would call her "neighbor."

The front door of the house opened, and Yvette Brandt walked out carrying a light jacket. "Hi, Cheyenne!" Her slim figure sported jeans and a green T-shirt. Even in her fifties, Yvette was a beautiful woman. She descended the three porch steps. "I think you're the first one to arrive. We're going to take the family minivan so we have plenty of room."

"Sounds good." Cheyenne smiled. "Thanks for inviting me."

Jake Brandt walked out of the house, pulling the front door shut behind him. "Looks like a beautiful day." He rounded the house toward the detached garage. "I'll pull out the minivan so you ladies can climb in easily."

"Thanks, honey." Yvette turned to Cheyenne. "I'm glad it's not raining. Jake and Derek got soaked last Friday afternoon at the rodeo."

"But the show goes on—rain or shine."

"Yes it does." Yvette placed her hand on Cheyenne's arm. "Oh, I wanted to tell you—this Friday is Tonya's birthday. We're planning a surprise party for her at our house at five o'clock. Can you come?"

"I'd love to. I know Tonya likes surprises."

"She does. We're planning it for five o'clock because she thinks she and Murray are just coming for dinner." Yvette smiled, creasing the crow's-feet by her eyes. "But the dinner will expand into a party, and the biggest surprise is that all her siblings will be here. We're turning it into a family reunion."

"Wow." *And I've been included!* "I'm sure you're looking forward to having all your children at home."

"Yes. I'm counting the days."

Jake pulled the minivan into the sunshine and parked. When he cut the engine, Cheyenne heard the sound of another car heading down the driveway. She recognized Lane's Mazda as it approached.

"Oh good. Callie and Lane are here." Yvette waved to them as they pulled up. "Now we just have to wait for Derek and Kandi." She walked to the minivan.

Cheyenne raised her eyebrows. *Kandi?* Derek must still be dating her.

A tiny pinprick of jealousy stabbed her, but she reminded herself that she had Rex.

Callie got out of the car and hugged Cheyenne. "I'm so glad you're coming with us, Chey. We're going to have so much fun today."

"I can't wait!" Cheyenne grinned. "I hope Lane doesn't mind if we run off to buy souvenirs."

"Yay for souvenirs!" Callie laughed. "That's the most fun thing about CFD to me. And don't worry about Lane. He wants to write a book about rodeos in America, so he'll be busy taking notes."

They walked together to the minivan.

"Hi, Mom." Callie hugged her. "Where's Derek?"

"He left about an hour ago to pick up Kandi." Yvette looked at her watch. "They should have been here by now. I hope they won't be too late."

Cheyenne ignored the clenching of her stomach as she followed Callie into the minivan. Lane was already sitting on the backseat in the corner, jotting a few thoughts in a small notebook, and they took seats next to him.

Girl time. That's how Cheyenne would frame this day, and Derek would be out of the picture.

⸎

Derek drove his pickup under the archway. As he crested the hill on the driveway, he noticed Mom and Dad, along with Lane, Callie, and Cheyenne, already sitting in the minivan.

Great! How long had they been waiting for them? He had been annoyed when Kandi called this morning at five thirty and asked him to pick her up. Bruce was supposed to drive her over, but Kandi claimed that Bruce's arthritis was bothering him. So Derek raced over to the MacKinnon ranch, only to discover that Kandi wasn't ready. He sat in their living room for twenty minutes trying to make small talk with Bruce.

Pulling over to the side of the driveway, Derek killed the engine. "Can you get your own door, Kandi? We need to hurry."

Without waiting for an answer, he grabbed his hat from the middle of the seat and strode toward the van. Kandi ran to his side. He paused to let her get in first. Amid a flurry of greetings, they sat on the empty middle seat. Lane, Callie, and Cheyenne sat in the back.

"Sorry we're late." Derek pulled the sliding door shut.

"That's okay." Dad threw the gears into DRIVE, and they started rolling. "We'll get some pancakes, no matter how long we have to wait in line."

❧

Derek adjusted his cowboy hat as he stood in line beside Kandi. He glanced at his watch. Almost seven. They had been standing for a half hour in the middle of the long line. Cheyenne Frontier Days claimed that ten thousand people ate at one of these free breakfasts, and as Derek looked back at the line that stretched four or five blocks, he figured they were right.

Mom and Dad stood beside him, with Kandi sticking to him like a burr under his saddle. She looked pretty today in jean shorts and a white peasant blouse, and her makeup was perfect. Most likely she had been painting her face while he waited for her at Bruce's house this morning. Derek folded his arms, no longer infatuated with her. If only he hadn't invited her to attend CFD with their family.

His glance bumped ahead about a half-dozen people to where Callie and Lane stood with Cheyenne. Somehow the three of them had gotten ahead in line. They laughed, and Cheyenne's musical laughter floated back to him. Derek grimaced, wishing he were standing with them—sans Kandi.

A few minutes after seven, the line began moving. Within fifteen minutes they were at the front, and Derek was handed a plate filled with pancakes and ham. He had to give credit to all those volunteers. They knew how to handle a crowd.

"Oh look at that!" Kandi pointed to the men who cooked the pancakes. They flipped them over their shoulders when they were done, and several boys ran behind the cooks, catching the flapjacks on large platters. She laughed. "I hope those kids don't miss."

A smile touched Derek's lips as he watched the boys. "I'm sure they'll throw away the ones that land on the ground."

"I hope so." Kandi turned to follow Mom and Dad.

Derek followed her, wishing he could somehow signal Mom to keep Kandi company. But she probably thought Kandi was his date. Obviously Callie and Cheyenne were going to hang around together all day, so that left Derek as Kandi's sole companion. He sighed.

It was going to be a long day.

* * *

In the arena, amid hundreds of other spectators, Cheyenne sat next to Callie on a white seat in the grandstand. "Those were good pancakes, and I'm actually full!" She gave a little laugh. "I hope my stomach's shrinking."

Callie lowered her voice. "You're doing great on your diet."

"Nine pounds so far." Cheyenne shook her head. "Just doesn't seem like much." She glanced down the row to her right. Lane sat on the other side of Callie. He pointed something out to Jake and Derek. All three men wore cowboy hats, and Yvette sported a pretty one made of straw. On the other side of Derek, Kandi listened as Yvette talked to her.

Cheyenne sighed. *What does Derek see in her?* Of course she was pretty and tiny, but Kandi didn't seem to have much of a personality.

But it doesn't matter. Today is girl time. With a smile, she inhaled deeply, smelling all those great smells of a rodeo—horses, leather, and the bodily scents, both good and bad, of the fans. She didn't need Derek to have a good time. *"This is the day which the Lord hath made; we will rejoice and be glad in it."*

"They're having barrel racing this morning." Callie motioned toward the center of the arena where three fifty-five-gallon barrels formed a large triangle on the mud of the arena floor. "When I was a little girl, I always dreamed of being a barrel racer. But I didn't have enough passion to be a good horse rider. I would rather sit in a corner and read a book."

Cheyenne looked at her. "I've only been on a horse one time. Remember?"

Callie laughed then covered her mouth with her fingers. "Sorry."

"It was your fault!" Cheyenne tried to hide a smile. "Why'd you let me ride bareback? I slid right off that animal, and it was a long way to the ground."

Callie giggled. "We were only ten years old, Chey. I didn't know you couldn't stay on a horse."

The announcer interrupted their memories, and the arena grew quiet as he announced the competition. A minute later, a brown horse thundered from the arena's alley. The female rider was dressed in jeans and a Western shirt, complete with cowboy boots and hat. The audience seemed to hold their collective breath as the cowgirl rounded the first barrel, raced over to the second one, rounded it, and galloped up to the third. Rounding that one, she raced back toward the point where she started.

Cheyenne leaned toward Callie. "That girl is skinny."

"Barrel racers have to be skinny. Think of the poor horse trying to race around the barrels with a big heavy person weighing him down."

Cheyenne laughed. "That's why I'm not a barrel racer, even if I could stay on a horse."

≈

Derek sat forward, leaning his arms on his thighs as he watched the barrel racer cross the finish line. Sitting back, he looked at his dad. "She almost nicked that third barrel with her foot."

"Yep. She needs to tighten her inside leg against the horse's flank."

The score flashed on the electronic board at the end of the arena.

"Nineteen point sixty-three seconds." Dad shook his head. "She's not going to win."

Derek glanced at Kandi who was looking down at her hands. Was she bored? *How can anyone be bored at a rodeo?* Mom talked to her sometimes, but Derek wasn't being fair to his mom if he let her carry the conversation. Since he had invited Kandi, he was responsible to see that she had a good time.

He sighed. "Ever see barrel racing before?"

"No." Her eyes met his. "It looks hard. When she rounded those barrels, the horse was almost sideways."

Derek adjusted his hat. "The faster, the better. It's actually dangerous, both for the horse and the rider. But those girls know what they're doing." He stopped as another cowgirl raced around the barrels.

When she crossed the finish line, Dad leaned toward him. "She was faster than that first gal."

The score flashed on the board.

"See there." Dad smiled. "Seventeen point ninety-eight seconds. She just might win."

Kandi cleared her throat. "How many barrel racers are there?"

Derek shrugged. "They usually have over a hundred."

"That many?" Her shoulders slumped.

He nodded. "This competition will last all morning." He pointed toward the arena. "Here comes another one."

The girl rounded the first barrel but was thrown from her

horse as she rounded the second one. In unison, the crowd rose to its feet. Several workers helped the girl up as the horse pranced off to the side.

Derek sat down with a relieved sigh. "She was going way too fast."

"Yep." Dad took his seat. "That little gal should have been more careful."

A half hour later, as another cowgirl successfully finished her race, Kandi leaned toward him. "Is there anything else we can do, Derek?"

He glanced at her. "Are you bored?"

She nodded, her mouth forming a little pout.

Derek glanced at his mom, but she had her eyes glued to the arena as another cowgirl galloped around. Barrel racing was Mom's favorite sport at the rodeo.

He waited until the score flashed on the board. Then he turned to Kandi. "Do you want to see the Old West Museum? They sell souvenirs there. Or we could wander around Wild Horse Gulch. That's like an old Western town. They sell merchandise, too, and even have people walking around dressed in nineteenth-century clothes."

She smiled. "Souvenirs first."

He stood, holding in a sigh. "Okay. Let's go."

She followed him down the grandstand and out into the sunshine. Dozens of people strolled along the sidewalk.

Derek took her to the museum, wishing he were back at the rodeo. He'd attended CFD since he was a boy, and he wasn't really interested in the museum or the town. But he would try to be interested for Kandi's sake.

At noon, after Kandi bought salt and pepper shakers shaped like a pair of boots as well as a CFD T-shirt, they met the others at the Oasis for lunch. Derek's mom, Callie, and Cheyenne placed food and bottles of water on a picnic table that was shaded by a huge red-and-white umbrella.

Mom looked up as they approached. "We bought hamburgers at the concession stand for everyone." She set a large box in the middle of the table. "Let's sit down and say grace."

Derek waited for Kandi to sit on the bench at the table then sat beside her. Dad asked the blessing. The table was quiet as everyone grabbed a hamburger and started eating.

Dad swallowed his first bite. "You two missed some excitement, son. One of the barrel racers really got hurt. I think they took her to the hospital."

Kandi shivered as she glanced at Derek. "I'm glad we weren't there."

Derek wished they *had* been there. "Who won the competition?"

"Some little gal way down the list." Dad grinned. "Her score was seventeen point four. She was fast! And she sure knew how to handle her horse."

"Oh man! I wish I could have seen that." Derek took a few more bites as the conversation drifted around him. He glanced down the table. Lane and Callie sat across on the other side with Cheyenne at the end. Derek nodded at his sister. "Did you stay for the entire competition?"

Callie leaned forward. "Most of it, but Cheyenne and I spent an hour at the Indian village. I bought some turquoise jewelry, and she bought an arrowhead necklace."

Kandi perked up. "I love Indian stuff! Where is the village?"

Callie pointed off in the distance. "It's over on the southeast corner of the park. We even saw a little show they put on by their dance group. They were decked out in their Indian garb and feathers, and their costumes were very colorful."

Kandi looked up at Derek. "Let's visit the Indian village after lunch."

He cocked an eyebrow. "You can visit it if you want to, but I'll be in the arena for the rest of the day to watch the cowboy contests."

"Oh." Kandi looked down.

Callie reached out to touch her hand. "I can take you over there. They have something special going on every hour.

We'll go to the arena first so we know where the family is sitting."

Kandi smiled at her. "Thanks."

With a relieved breath, Derek added his smile of thanks to his sister. Hopefully that would take care of Kandi for the rest of the afternoon.

❧

In the grandstand, even though a lot of people conversed in the rows in front of her and behind her, Cheyenne sat in the Brandt row by herself. Jake and Lane had decided to get some soft drinks, and Callie had just left with Kandi and Yvette for the Indian village. Cheyenne should have gone with them—the walking would have helped her lose weight. But she would rather sit and watch the cowboy contests.

Feeling someone sit down beside her, she looked to her left. Her eyes met Derek's, and her pulse quickened.

"Hey, Cheyenne. Sitting here all by yourself?" He held a can of cola and took a quick swig.

She leaned away from him. "I already spent all my money on souvenirs, so I plan to stay in the arena and watch the cowboys all afternoon."

He grinned. "Good choice."

Cheyenne looked out at the arena. She wasn't going to let her heart beat a second faster over the guy sitting next to her. "How's the ranch doing, Derek?"

"Right now things are going well, but did you hear what happened two weeks ago?" When she shook her head, he continued. "Wolves broke through our fence and killed fourteen sheep."

She gasped. "Oh that's terrible!"

He nodded. "Three ewes and eleven lambs. Dad and I found the break in the fence where they got in, but we've never caught the wolves."

"How do you know they were wolves? They could have been coyotes."

"No." Derek adjusted his hat. "Those lambs were brought

down by dispersers—young males trying to establish their own territory. And they didn't eat the sheep, they just broke their necks." He sighed. "That's the way wolves operate."

"Those poor little lambs." Tears crept to her eyes. "I'm so sorry that happened, Derek. That's a loss of income for you, isn't it?"

"Yeah, but we'll recover." Derek eyed her a moment then looked up beyond her.

Cheyenne turned her head as Jake took the seat next to her. Lane sat down beside him.

"Howdy." Jake held a large cup of cola in his hand. "Did the other girls already leave for the Indian village?"

"Yep, they're sightseeing." Cheyenne twirled a strand of blond hair between her fingers. "I think they'll be gone most of the afternoon."

Jake grunted. "Why would they want to miss the rodeo?"

Derek leaned over her to talk to his dad. "Kandi's not into rodeos, even though she told me she wanted to see the cowboy contests." With a little shrug, he sat back and slid down a few inches in his seat.

Cheyenne glanced at him before looking out at the arena. Evidently Derek was disappointed that Kandi wasn't sitting beside him right now. *He really must like that girl.* Instead here he was, sitting next to Cheyenne.

I'll treat him like I would treat my brother.

She'd never had a brother, but she could pretend, couldn't she? *Call me Callie.*

Derek's shoulder bumped hers. "Saddle bronc is next. It's one of my favorites."

"I like saddle bronc and bareback bronc, but not bull riding."

"You've got to be kidding!" He stared at her as if she were crazy. "Everyone loves bull riding."

"That's *my* favorite." Jake nodded. "Those bull riders are really talented—and fearless."

"They have to be." She frowned. "It's dangerous to hop on a live bull!"

They both laughed, and Jake turned to Lane with a comment.

Derek sat up and leaned toward her. "That's true, Cheyenne, but all of these events are dangerous. Even barrel racing."

"Yeah. I saw that girl go down." She shook her head. "Why would anyone want to risk her life? But the cowboys are the real daredevils. Did they start bronc riding for the challenge? Man against animal?"

"Bronco busting started when cowboys had to break in wild horses. They competed with each other to see who could ride with the most style." Derek motioned toward the arena. "Now they have all kinds of rules, and they have to stay on at least eight seconds, or they'll be disqualified."

"Why would anyone want to do that? It's so dangerous."

He grinned. "I'd have to agree with you there. The life of a cowboy is not as glamorous as some people think, but it sure is fun to watch the competitions."

The announcer's voice came over the loudspeaker, introducing the event. In a few minutes, the first rider jumped out of the chute on the back of a bucking bronco. The man held to a rope with his right hand, and his cowboy boots pushed out the saddle's stirrups as he bounced up and down.

Derek placed his arm around the back of her chair, his eyes never straying from the cowboy. "Notice how he waves his left hand in the air." He spoke in a hushed voice as if he didn't want to break the cowboy's concentration, although the man would never hear him. "He can't touch anything with his free hand."

Cheyenne already knew that, having attended quite a few rodeos during her lifetime, but her heartbeat took off at Derek's nearness. She glanced at his profile, just inches away, as he watched the rider. His dark eyes, his straight nose, his perfect lips—a face that must be twenty years younger than Rex's weathered one.

His straight, slim fingers pointed to the arena. "Leaning so far back in the saddle helps him stay on and keeps his feet in the stirrups. If either foot slips out or he drops the buck rein, he'll be disqualified." The cowboy fell off the bucking horse into the mud, and Derek turned to her. Their gazes locked, and Cheyenne's scalp prickled. His gaze dropped to her lips, just like it did more than three weeks ago in his truck, before he looked back at her eyes.

The hint of a smile touched his lips before he pulled his arm from her seat and sat back. "I think he made the eight seconds. We'll see what his score is."

A small sigh escaped as Cheyenne's pulse returned to normal. Why didn't she have that kind of emotional interaction with Rex? She had tried to gaze into his eyes and work up her emotions, but the chemistry just wasn't there.

But why was Derek acting like this? Wasn't he dating Kandi? Was he two-timing her?

"If you can't be with the one you love, love the one you're with."

The old saying popped into Cheyenne's head. She remembered some girls at college spouting off those words and laughing about it, but Cheyenne never thought it was funny.

Now she was experiencing it with Derek Brandt! And she didn't like it, not one bit.

twelve

On Friday evening, Derek sat in the living room along with the entire Brandt family. They watched collectively as Tonya tore the birthday paper off her last gift.

Derek had purposely taken a seat beside Cheyenne on the sofa, and she had looked startled when he sat down—the same look she gave him at CFD when he sat next to her in the grandstand. He grinned to himself. He certainly enjoyed sitting next to her during the saddle-bronc contests, and he couldn't believe that "electrical moment" they shared.

But Cheyenne had seemed distant. She frequently conversed with Dad and Lane during the rest of the competition, and she seemed relieved when the women arrived later to sit with them. Then, for the remainder of the day, she paid absolutely no attention to him.

She must really like Rex Pierson.

Derek's brother, Ryan, pulled a straight-back chair from the dining room and set it beside the sofa. Derek was thankful he had someone to talk to. After Cheyenne's initial reaction, she turned her back on him and talked to Callie, who was sitting next to her.

Across the room, Tonya sat in the blue chair with Murray perched on the arm. Mom and Dad sat on the love seat, and most of Derek's siblings sat beside their spouses on chairs they had pulled from the dining room. His two little nephews played with building blocks on the floor.

Tonya held up a DVD. "Oh! *The Quiet Man.* I love old movies. Thanks, Callie." She turned to her husband. "Do we have this one, Murray?"

"Nope." Twitch grinned. "Callie asked me last week."

Tonya smiled as her glance swung around the room. "I

can't believe you guys planned a surprise party behind my back. Thank you so much for all the presents. This has to be the greatest family in the world."

"It is." Dad glanced at Mom. "God has been good to us, hasn't He, honey?"

"He certainly has." Mom smiled as she looked around. "The Lord gave us six wonderful children, five children-in-law, and two grandchildren."

Melissa leaned forward. "With more on the way."

This announcement precipitated an outburst of exclamations. Melissa was quickly surrounded by the women of the family. Most of the men stood and shook Philip's hand.

Since Cheyenne stayed seated, Derek kept his seat beside her, but he caught his brother-in-law's eye. "Congratulations, Phil."

"Thanks." Philip smiled as he took a step toward Derek. "Would you believe—her due date is two days after her birthday. Melissa is hoping the baby's early so they'll be exactly thirty years apart."

"Thirty years." Derek nodded. "Wow."

Philip turned away as Ryan claimed his attention.

Derek heard a quiet sniff beside him, and he turned in time to see Cheyenne wipe a tear from her eye. Compassion filled him, and he leaned toward her. "You okay?"

She nodded, but a tear rolled down her cheek. She covered her face with her hands.

"Cheyenne?" Barely thinking what he was doing, Derek put his arms around her and pulled her close to him. "What's wrong?"

With her face still in her hands, she just shook her head, but after a few seconds she leaned toward him, and a few quiet sobs escaped between her fingers. He tightened his grip, smelling the sweet fragrance of her hair, and a surge of protectiveness swept through him.

Ryan came back to claim his seat. Frowning, he glanced at Cheyenne in Derek's arms. "Is she okay?"

Suddenly she straightened, causing Derek's arms to slip

away. "I'm fine." She wiped her fingers under her eyes as she stood. "Excuse me."

Derek watched her walk out of the room before turning to Ryan. "I have no idea what's wrong with her."

Ryan lowered his voice. "That happens with women sometimes. Puzzling, if you ask me." Raising his hands, he gave a little shrug.

Derek just nodded, still concerned. Should he follow Cheyenne? See if she was all right?

"Well." Ryan motioned toward Melissa. "It's about time someone else in the family has kids besides Holly and me."

"Mom and Dad will probably have a bunch of grandkids in the next few years." All Derek's siblings were married now—everyone except him.

He glanced at the door where Cheyenne had disappeared. If only she was still in his arms.

⁂

"Let me grab some clothes for tomorrow." Derek poked his head in his closet and pulled out a pair of jeans and a T-shirt.

Holly, his sister-in-law, smiled up at him as she changed her younger son's clothes. "Thanks for giving up your bedroom for us, Derek. We appreciate it."

"No problem. I can sleep on the sofa for one night."

He stepped over his nephew Peter. The three-year-old pushed Matchbox cars across the wooden floor as he made motor noises.

Ryan entered the room, pulling one suitcase behind him and carrying a duffel bag. "I have to make another trip out to the car for that stuff in the backseat." His brown eyes glanced at his wife. "Do you need anything else?"

"No." Holly picked up Paul. "Just the diaper bag and that box of things for your mom."

"I'll help you." Derek laid his clothes on the bed and descended the stairs behind his brother.

They walked out the front door and into the warm night air.

Ryan opened the back door of his car. "I can't believe tomorrow's August first."

"I know." Derek took the large diaper bag he was handed. "This summer is whizzing by. Next weekend I'm scheduled to go to Yellowstone."

"Really?" Ryan straightened and closed the car door. "Are Mom and Dad going, too?"

"No, it's for the children's home in Casper. They're sending the kids on a field trip with volunteers so the staff can have the weekend off." Derek turned toward the house and fell in step beside his brother. "We have three going from our church—Cheyenne, Kandi, and me."

"Who's Kandi?"

"A girl I dated. She's—"

"You? Dating?" Ryan stopped. "Get out of here! You've never dated a girl in your life."

Derek leaned against the porch rail. "Is there some rule that I can't go out with a girl?"

"I'm not saying it's bad." Ryan set his box on the porch floor. "I'm just surprised. Ever since you were fifteen, you said you weren't getting married until you're forty. And I happen to know that you don't like change."

"I don't." Derek dropped the diaper bag down to the floor. "Actually, I'm not dating Kandi anymore."

Ryan frowned. "Why not?"

Derek gave a shrug. "She's not my type. I'm not sure about marriage anyway. That would be a huge change in my life, and I don't know if I'll ever be ready for it."

"It is a big adjustment and a big responsibility, especially when you have kids. But I wouldn't trade it for anything. I love my family." Ryan quirked an eyebrow at him. "What about Cheyenne? You two looked rather cozy. Did she ever tell you why she was crying?"

"No." Derek folded his arms. "Cheyenne's not interested in me. She's dating Rex Pierson, our new neighbor, and it looks like they're headed toward marriage."

"Too bad. You and Cheyenne would make a great couple."

Derek grimaced. "I know, although to be honest, I've been struggling with God's will. Sometimes I think God wants me to remain single so I can serve Him." He spread out his hands. "Next weekend I can go to Yellowstone to help out without worrying about leaving a family back home."

Ryan shrugged. "If that's what the Lord wants you to do, that's great. But don't forget the old saying, 'Charity begins at home.' I want to raise my children to be the next generation of Christians for Christ's kingdom. I get to have an impact on my own family, which is a lot more than just a once-in-a-while charity thing for strangers."

"I suppose that's true."

"I'll keep you in prayer." Ryan laid his hand on Derek's shoulder. "Whatever you do, make sure that it's God's will, not your own."

"Thanks, bro." Derek picked up the diaper bag and followed Ryan into the house. He liked the thought of raising the next generation of Christians.

But he couldn't think of one girl he wanted to marry—at least not one *available* girl.

thirteen

Cheyenne walked in the back door and released Marshal from the leash. "Dad? Are you home?"

That was a dumb question since his car was parked in the driveway. But it was only six o'clock on Saturday evening. Usually he wasn't home from Wilkins Grocery until eight thirty.

He walked into the kitchen. "Hi, baby girl. I'm on my way out again."

She raised her eyebrows at her father's attire. "A dress shirt and slacks?"

He turned to face her and patted his stomach. "Does this look okay?"

"Well, you can't go wrong with blue and tan. Where are you going, Dad?"

He lifted his keys from the hook by the door. "Didn't I tell you?"

"Obviously not." Cheyenne folded her arms as she leaned against the counter.

"Well. . ." A smile crept to his face. "I have a date tonight."

Cheyenne's jaw dropped. "A date? You?"

"Yes, me." He dropped his keys and stooped to retrieve them. "Don't you think a woman could find your old man attractive?" He straightened up with a grunt.

"It's not that, Dad." She rolled her eyes. "What woman could resist you? I'm just surprised, that's all." *Stunned* would be a better word. "Uh, who is she?"

"Janet Oliver."

Cheyenne's right eyebrow hiked up on its own accord. "Mrs. Oliver? Uh, that's great, Dad." *I can't believe it!* "She's. . . a nice lady." *My dad is dating Janet Oliver!*

He just grinned. Jiggling the keys in his hand, he turned toward the door. "Guess I'll be off."

"Wait! How did this come about? When did you ask her out?"

He turned back. "Janet dropped by last night when you were at Tonya's party. She played the piano, which she said is badly out of tune, and then we had a good talk." Leaning against the door, he sighed. "I don't know if you remember this, but your mom and Janet were the best of friends when she lived in Fort Lob."

Cheyenne thought back. "I do have a distinct memory of her being here when I was little. We were eating lunch, and Mrs. Oliver and Mom were talking about me starting kindergarten soon."

He nodded. "After you started school, Janet came over for lunch almost every day, or your mom would go to her house. Sometimes they went shopping." His eyebrows pulled into a frown. "A couple years later when your mom got sick, Janet sat with her and read the Bible, especially toward the end. When Lynn died, she really grieved." He shook his head. "She was really good to Lynn, and I'll always be grateful for that."

With his gaze on the floor, Dad seemed to have forgotten that Cheyenne was standing there.

She cleared her throat. "So you're just taking Janet out as an old friend? I mean—this is just a friendship date, right? Not a serious looking-for-a-spouse date?" She bit her lip, hoping she hadn't overstepped some imaginary boundary.

Dad cocked his head. "It might turn into something serious. I need to find God's will for my future just as you do for yours."

"I know, Dad." She placed her hand on his arm. "Well. . . whatever happens, I hope you and Janet have a good time tonight."

He smiled. "Thanks. We will." Turning, he pulled open the door and walked out.

Cheyenne watched as he got in the car and drove away. She looked down at Marshal who was resting in his doggybed. "Do you think Janet will end up as my stepmother?" She took a deep breath. "That would be so weird."

On the other hand, maybe Janet could spice up Dad's wardrobe. At least she'd never let him wear a pink-flowered tie with his brown plaid suit coat.

Hmm. . . Janet and Dad. "That might be good. Dad won't be alone after I get married."

Her goal was to marry Rex by the end of the year—a December wedding, or January at the latest. That would leave a year and a half to have a baby before her thirtieth birthday.

And Grandmother's millions would be hers.

She sank into a chair at the kitchen table. "I feel so. . . greedy!"

Marshal cocked his head at her.

"Do I really want to get married just to get that money? I could be miserable my whole life!" Folding her arms on the table, she laid her head down with a sigh.

In the quiet, she heard her cell phone ring in the bedroom. Walking back, she picked it up and looked at the ID. *Rex.*

She opened her phone, anticipating his deep voice. She hadn't seen Rex since Thursday evening when he waited for her to lock up the post office and took her to supper at the Cattlemen's Diner. That date was becoming a common occurrence in their relationship.

"Hi, Rex!"

"Howdy, darlin'. How've you been?"

"Great! How is the ranch coming along?"

"Well now, I just about have everything squared away. Got the ol' bunkhouse cleaned out and have three hired hands livin' there. One of 'em is a really good wrangler, but I don't have no horses." He stopped to chuckle. "My hundred head of cattle seem content with their new place. Had to get the plumbing fixed in the house, but the pipes are in good shape now." He took a deep breath. "Anyways, I feel like I can finally breathe."

She smiled. "That's good." She never noticed before how much he sounded like a country bumpkin.

"Yeah. I'll probably be tied up here all next week workin' the ranch, but ya wanna go out on Friday? It'll be kinda like a celebration."

"Not on Friday, Rex. I'll be at Yellowstone next weekend."

"Oh yeah. Forgot about that." He paused. "How about Thursday then? We can make a night of it in Lusk with a dinner and movie."

Yes! Somewhere besides the Cattlemen's Diner. "I like that idea. There's a restaurant in Lusk called Mama's Kitchen. They serve Italian food, and it's really good."

"Okay, we'll go there. How about I pick you up at the post office at five on Thursday?"

She smiled. "I'm looking forward to it. And I'll see you tomorrow morning in church, right?"

"Yep, church tomorrow morning." He paused. "Night, darlin'."

"Good-bye, Rex."

With a sigh, she closed the phone. *Darlin'.* At least Rex liked her, and he was taking things slow, not rushing into an intimate relationship. But it still bothered her that they had no chemistry.

Her thoughts shot back to Tonya's birthday party last night. Melissa's announcement hit her so hard. She suddenly realized how much she wanted to have a baby.

Whether she got the four million or not.

❧

Cheyenne stopped at the front door and turned to Rex with a smile. "Thanks for the great time. I really enjoyed that movie."

"Me, too." The reflection from the porch light pricked his eyes, and his face wrinkled up with his smile. "But I enjoyed going out with a pretty lady more."

Before Cheyenne could reply, he cupped her face in his calloused hands. His lips met hers in a kiss that lasted for a few seconds. He lifted his head then kissed her again.

He stepped back. "Night, darlin'." He winked.

"Bye." Cheyenne waited as he walked off the porch. He got in his truck and started it in a cloud of fumes, then waved to her. She waved back.

This is not good. Not only was there no passion, but she didn't even enjoy his kisses.

Cheyenne blew out a breath. What could she do?

She only had two choices—give up the inheritance or try to fall in love with Rex Pierson.

fourteen

Behind the wheel in his pickup, Derek was thankful when the orphanage in Casper came into view. It was Friday, August 7, the weekend for the Yellowstone National Park outing. Early this morning, he met Cheyenne and Kandi at the church in Fort Lob and gave them a ride to Casper. Kandi had scampered up into the truck cab first, beating out Cheyenne, whom Derek wished was sitting beside him. As usual Kandi didn't say much, so Derek and Cheyenne ended up carrying on the conversation around her.

"Here we are, ladies." In the orphanage driveway, he pulled up behind two fifteen-passenger vans, threw the gears in Park, and turned off the engine.

Cheyenne gazed up at the huge house. "Wow, it's a mansion. The columns in the front make it look so stately."

Derek leaned forward to look at her across Kandi. "You've never visited the children's home before, Cheyenne?"

"No. I've never even heard of it." Her blue eyes met his. "And it's been here for thirty years?"

"Yep. Started by Frank and Grace Lindley. I usually come once a month and do some activities with the children as a volunteer."

"Oh, I'd love to do that." Cheyenne smiled. "Let me know the next time you come."

He grinned. "I will."

Kandi sat silently during this exchange, turning her head to look at each speaker as if she was at a ping-pong match.

Derek glanced out the windshield. "Here comes Mr. Lindley." He opened the door and exited the truck, looking forward to the day at Yellowstone.

❧

Cheyenne watched a tall, bearded man descend the porch

steps. He held a piece of paper in one hand and was dressed in a short-sleeved gray shirt and dark slacks. Cheyenne opened the passenger door and climbed out of the cab. Kandi followed her. They joined Derek in front of the truck.

Mr. Lindley stretched out his right hand. "Derek! Good to see you again."

Derek shook his hand. "Hi, Mr. Lindley." He turned and motioned to the girls. "This is Kandi MacKinnon and Cheyenne Wilkins."

"Thanks for volunteering to go with us." Mr. Lindley's handshake was firm as he took Cheyenne's hand, and his dark eyes twinkled when he smiled. He reminded her of Professor Bhaer in *Little Women.*

She returned his smile. "This trip sounds fun. I'm looking forward to it."

"Um, me, too." Kandi nodded.

"Good, good." Mr. Lindley took a pair of reading glasses from his shirt pocket and looked at his paper. "You will each be in charge of two children. Let's see. Kandi, you will have two girls." He glanced at her over his glasses. "Madeline is eight years old, and Rayna is six. They're good children. I'm sure you'll have no problem with them."

Kandi just nodded.

He looked back at the paper. "Cheyenne, you'll be in charge of two boys."

"Boys?"

Mr. Lindley shrugged. "We have more boys than girls, and we have a lot of women volunteers." He looked down. "These two are both five years old. Arthur and Noah."

Cheyenne frowned. "Will I share the same cabin with them overnight?"

The director looked at her over his glasses. "If you were the boys' mother or housemother you could, but since you're not. . ." His over-the-rim gaze switched to Derek. "I'll have them stay overnight with you, Derek. You'll also be in charge of Nathan and Joshua."

"Nathan, huh?" Derek pursed his lips.

Mr. Lindley placed a fatherly hand on Derek's shoulder. "You can handle him. Besides, Nathan likes you, whether he shows it or not."

Another car pulled into the driveway, and Mr. Lindley waved at them. "More of my volunteers. We'll leave for Yellowstone in about fifteen minutes." He walked to the other car.

Placing his hands on his hips, Derek looked at Cheyenne. "I guess I'll end up with four boys."

"Only at night. I want to watch my two during the day."

Kandi sidled up to Derek. "We can all hang out together, can't we?"

"Yeah, we can do that." He walked to the back of his truck.

Cheyenne glanced at Kandi, who looked lonely standing by herself. Suddenly she felt sorry for the girl. "Don't worry, Kandi." She smiled at her. "We'll all stick together and have a good time this weekend."

"Okay." Kandi smiled back, and that smile transformed her entire countenance.

She really is a pretty girl. No wonder Derek was taken with her.

❧

That afternoon, Cheyenne breathed in the warm air as a "covered wagon" bumped along the uneven ground toward the Rosey cookout near Tower Falls. She sat on a padded bench seat between Arthur and Noah. The orphans, as Mr. Lindley unabashedly called them, filled the long yellow wagon. A cowboy named Mitch held the reins of the two horses, and the wagon had canvas awnings tied up against the roof. The murmur of conversation surrounded them.

"When are we gonna eat?"

Looking down to her right, Cheyenne met the blue eyes of Arthur. "When we get to the cookout, we'll eat. I hear they're serving steak. That sounds good, doesn't it?"

"Yeah. I'm hungry. Can we have seconds, too?"

She raised her eyebrows. Arthur didn't fit her perception of a poor orphan. Although he was taller than most five-year-olds, he probably weighed fifteen pounds more, with a roly-poly body and chunky arms and legs. A thatch of blond hair topped his chubby face.

Cheyenne cleared her throat. "Are you sure you need a second helping?" She lowered her voice. "Did you know that I'm on a diet, Arthur? I want to lose a few more pounds. At the cookout, I'm only going to eat what's on my plate. Maybe you should do that, too."

"But why?" His light blond eyebrows formed a V in the middle of his forehead. "Just 'cause I'm fat? I'm not worried about being fat. 'Big is beautiful.' My mom always used to say that. She was a fat person, too."

"Was she?" Cheyenne tried to hide her smile.

Arthur frowned. "What does it mean, Miss Anne?"

"My name is *Cheyenne*, not Miss Anne."

"But what does 'big is beautiful' mean?"

"Well. . ." Cheyenne thought a moment. "Maybe your mom was trying to accept herself the way she was instead of trying to change."

"I like myself just the way I am." He grinned. "Big is beautiful, right?"

"Right!" With a laugh, Cheyenne put up her hand. "Give me five!"

Arthur smiled as he slapped her hand.

She glanced down to her left at her other little charge. Noah's small brown head bent over two round magnets. He concentrated on keeping as little space between them as possible before they snapped together.

Amid the hum of conversation in the wagon, she heard Derek's voice way in the back. "Hey, everyone! Bison on the left!"

The heads of counselors and children turned that direction. A hundred yards away, five humpbacked shaggy animals ate grass like cows.

"Wow! They're big!" Arthur leaned against Cheyenne. "What are they?"

She glanced down at him. "Bison. Some people call them buffalo."

"Oh." Arthur nodded. "I know what a buffalo is."

Derek's strong voice reached over the wagon. "A herd of deer! Over on the right!"

Everyone's head turned that way.

"Look at that." Cheyenne pointed to the three deer that were leaping away from the wagon. "Don't they run fast?"

Arthur nodded. "They're cool."

"More bison!" Derek's voice again.

With a grin, Cheyenne turned around and raised her voice. "Are you the self-appointed tour guide, Derek?"

From the back bench he gave her a thumbs-up. "Hey, I've been to Yellowstone before."

Cheyenne turned to the front, wishing she hadn't looked back. Derek's two boys sat on his left, and on his right Kandi MacKinnon stuck to his side. She seemed to be paying more attention to him than she was to the two little girls who sat beside her.

A sigh slipped between Cheyenne's lips. She thought of her date with Rex last night, and his good-night kisses. If that man had been Derek. . .

Lord, help me to accept my circumstances as they are. She would learn a lesson from Arthur's mom.

Noah lifted his brown eyes to meet Cheyenne's blue ones. "Are we almost there?"

"I'm not sure." Taking his small hand in hers, she gave it a quick squeeze. Noah hadn't said more than a few words, and she wondered if he had lost his parents recently. "But we'll be at the Rosey cookout soon enough. Then we can eat."

Arthur leaned against her. "I really am hungry."

"You told me." She smiled at him as she tucked a strand of hair behind her ear.

"Hey!" Arthur jumped up. "I think I see the cookout place. We're almost there, Miss Anne."

"It's *Cheyenne*." She looked ahead. Between the trees, she

spotted several long picnic tables. "Yep. Looks like we've arrived."

She smiled, determined to forget about her relationship woes this weekend. She would "mother" these two sweet boys God had placed in her care.

❧

It was dark that evening when Cheyenne unlocked the Lake Lodge cabin and opened the door. "Okay girls, here we are." She flipped the switch inside, and the overhead light came on.

Stepping over the threshold, she glanced around as she set down her duffel bag. The small room was furnished with a double bed and a table with two chairs. Through the thin wall on the left, she could hear the exclamations of their neighbors—another group of girls.

Kandi walked inside and frowned. "How. . .primitive." Her two charges, Rayna and Madeline, dropped their sleeping bags on the floor.

Rayna smiled, showing the gap in her teeth. "Cool."

"Yeah. I like it." Madeline's ponytail bobbed as she nodded her head.

"That's good." Cheyenne walked to a small window. "The room is clean, but it's a little stuffy in here. Let's open the window." After a couple of tugs, she succeeded in sliding it open. A cool evening breeze brushed past her. "Ah! That feels good." She turned back to the room.

The little girls knelt on the wooden floor to spread open their sleeping bags, but Kandi still stood by the door. Her hand rested on the handle of her suitcase, and a frown rested on her face.

Cheyenne took a deep breath. She *would* get stuck sharing a room with Kandi MacKinnon—with a double bed of all things! *Lord, help me to have a good attitude.* She smiled at the two girls on the floor. "You girls have the right idea. We might as well call it a night and get ready for bed."

With a sigh, Kandi rolled her suitcase to the double bed and opened a narrow door in the wall. "At least we have a bathroom. I hope the shower has plenty of hot water. I feel grimy after being outdoors all day."

"Um. . .Kandi, why don't you let the girls use the bathroom first? Then they can get to sleep."

Kandi plunked down on the bed. "Okay."

Cheyenne raised her eyebrows. "Uh. . .are you going to help them?" She didn't mind helping the girls, but they were supposed to be in Kandi's charge, not hers.

"We can do it ourselves." Madeline pulled a pair of pajamas from her backpack. "When Mrs. Lindley tells us to get ready for bed, we know what to do."

Cheyenne smiled at her. "You are very grown-up."

With a sigh, Kandi took off her left shoe and rubbed her foot. "I'll be glad when we can get back to civilization."

Cheyenne unzipped her duffel bag. *Give me patience, Lord!*

⁂

Cheyenne shifted on the mattress, turning on her side away from Kandi. Outside the window several crickets chirped. She listened to the even breathing of the two little girls on the floor. Her eyes drifted shut.

"Cheyenne."

At her whispered name, she startled awake. "Yes?"

"I have a question about Derek."

Great! Cheyenne turned over to face the middle of the bed. "What's your question?"

"I was just thinking about when Derek and I get married."

When! Cheyenne's heart thudded. "I didn't know the two of you were engaged."

"We're not." Kandi gave a high-pitched giggle. "But I'm sure it will happen. Woman's intuition, you know."

Was that all Kandi was going on?

"Anyway, do you know how many children Derek wants?"

In the dark, Cheyenne rolled her eyes. "Uh, knowing Derek, he would say children are cheaper by the dozen. He'll probably adopt twelve."

"Did you say *adopt?*"

Cheyenne tried not to laugh at the incredulous sound in Kandi's voice. She cleared her throat. "He volunteers at the orphanage every month, doesn't he? I bet he'll have two or three orphans living with him by the time you guys get married."

"All right. Now I know you're kidding." Kandi gave a little grunt. "I hope he doesn't want to adopt. I sure don't. I want to have my own kids."

"Yeah, so do I." *By the time I'm thirty!* "But there's nothing wrong with adoption. I already love those two boys I watched today. That little Arthur is so cute. I would adopt him in a heartbeat."

"Are you serious?"

Arthur's round face popped into her mind, and she realized it was true. "Yes I am. I would love to adopt him."

"That is crazy."

Arthur. What would it be like to be his mother? He had blond hair and blue eyes, as she did. He was tall for his age, as she had been. He was chubby, as she still was—unfortunately.

Kandi yawned. "We'd better get to sleep. Good night, Cheyenne."

" 'Night." Cheyenne rolled back on her side. She smiled to herself as she thought of Arthur saying "Big is beautiful." But then her smile faded. Rex said he wanted children, but what if he didn't want to adopt Arthur? Adoptions were expensive. Of course, they could wait until Cheyenne inherited her grandmother's money in a couple of years. But what if Rex said no? Or what if someone else adopted Arthur?

Lord, I would love to adopt that little boy. She prayed for a few more minutes, asking God to place that desire in her future husband's heart, too. A gentle peace filled her soul, and she drifted off to sleep.

fifteen

The next afternoon, Derek stood in the back of the group beside his two boys, and Joshua, the ten-year-old, leaned against his left side. Derek threw his arm around the boy and squeezed his shoulder. "Ready to see Old Faithful blow its top, Joshua?"

The hazel eyes looked up into his. "I've never seen a geyser before."

"There's a first time for everything." Derek glanced beyond Joshua to Nathan, his other charge. Nathan was a typical twelve-year-old—rebellious. But beyond that, Nathan seemed to be jaded by life. That boy's attitude had been a problem since Derek met him a year ago.

Cheyenne stood in front of Derek with Arthur and Noah. Kandi's two girls stood with them as Cheyenne pointed at the steam from the geyser that floated off in the wind. Instead of standing next to her girls, Kandi planted herself beside Derek. He wished she would take her duties as a counselor more seriously. She didn't seem to care about the kids at all.

The crowd quieted as the geyser started, and the water went up a foot then stopped. The steam wafted off to the right.

"False start." Derek looked to his left. "Do you know what makes the geyser blow, Nathan?"

The boy gave him a dark look before he shrugged. "Is this like science class or something?"

"No, it's like me asking you why a geyser shoots up." He glanced from Nathan to Joshua, who looked at him with interest. "Do you know, Joshua?"

He shook his head.

Derek pointed toward the geyser. "Deep underground the water is heated—"

"Skip the science lesson." Folding his arms, Nathan looked away.

"Hey, buddy. You might need to know this someday."

Nathan turned back with a frown. "Why?"

"Well. . ." Derek lowered his voice. "Let's say you started liking a really pretty girl, and your class went on a field trip to Yellowstone. What if you wanted to impress her?"

Derek reached out and tapped Cheyenne's shoulder. She turned around, her clear blue eyes meeting his. *And she sure is pretty.*

He glanced back at Nathan. "If I wanted to impress Cheyenne with how smart I was, I would tell her that water heats deep below the surface by very hot rocks to a boiling temperature." He looked around, realizing he had an audience. Not only were Nathan and Joshua listening, but Cheyenne and the other children stared at him with rapt attention. Kandi folded her arms, as if she didn't like him using Cheyenne for the pretty-girl illustration.

Kandi would just have to get over it.

"That boiling water soon changes to steam. And steam rises. Right?" He glanced around, and several heads nodded. "Okay. Then the steam pushes the water above it up toward the surface. When the steam suddenly expands, it pushes the water out the geyser with great force." Clapping his hands together, he lifted them as he made a whooshing sound.

Cheyenne's blue eyes widened. "Oh! So that's how it happens." She looked at the children surrounding her. "Isn't Mr. Derek smart? I'm impressed."

He grinned at her before turning to Nathan. "See? I knew I could impress a pretty girl."

Nathan actually smiled. Derek squeezed his shoulder before glancing around. His eyes met Kandi's.

She wasn't smiling.

"Look, everyone!" Cheyenne pointed toward the geyser.

A column of water, cloudy with steam, shot up about 120 feet in the air.

"There she blows!" Derek looked down at Joshua. "Now you can say you've seen Old Faithful in action."

The children were silent as the geyser held their attention. When the show was over, Mr. Lindley walked in front of the group.

"That was awesome, wasn't it?" With a smile, he raised his bushy eyebrows as he nodded at several children. "There's a lot of power in that water, and it's really hot." He motioned toward the wooden boardwalk behind them. "Right now we're going to stroll along the boardwalk. You'll see all kinds of geysers and boiling pools in this area. Stay with your leader, and don't step off the walkway."

"Hear that, men?" Derek smiled at Nathan and Joshua. "Let's go."

The two boys followed the others as all the children and counselors turned and started down the path. Derek brought up the rear.

Kandi stayed by his side. "I'll walk with you, Derek."

He frowned. "You're supposed to be with your girls."

"Cheyenne has them." Kandi motioned up ahead. Sure enough, Cheyenne strolled along the boardwalk with Kandi's two girls as well as her two boys. Cheyenne talked to the children, holding the hand of one of the girls. They didn't seem to miss Kandi.

Derek shook his head. "I think you'd better go up there."

"But I need to talk to you."

He sighed. "What do you need to talk about?"

"Did you like your cabin last night? I thought ours was kind of primitive."

Is this what she needs to talk about? He blew out a breath. "Were you expecting a five-star hotel?"

"No, but it was so. . .basic."

"You don't know what *basic* is, Kandi. Camping in tents is basic. Those cabins were nice, I thought."

She walked beside him in silence for a moment. "Cheyenne and I had a good talk."

He hesitated, but curiosity got the best of him. "What did you talk about?"

"Well. . .we were talking about children, and she said she would adopt one of those orphans in a heartbeat if she could." Kandi frowned. "She meant Arthur."

"Wow." *Good for you, Cheyenne!* "That's cool."

"I think it's crazy. When I get mar—" She shook her head. "Never mind. But then we talked about someone else." Leaning toward him, she grabbed his hand and squeezed. "You."

"Me?" With a frown, Derek disengaged his hand and thrust it in his pocket. Kandi was coming on a little too strong. "You know, I really think you should walk with Rayna and Madeline. Mr. Lindley put you in charge of those two girls."

Her lips formed into a pout, but Kandi turned and jogged ahead to join Cheyenne and the children. Derek slowly let out a sigh. Why couldn't that girl take a hint and leave him alone?

Nathan turned around and grinned at him. "I guess you told her, huh, Derek?"

Great! He should have figured the two boys in front of him would hear every word of their conversation. "Girls are hard to figure sometimes, Nathan." *Which is why I should remain single.*

Derek looked out at the barren land as they walked. The wooden boardwalk cut a path through the sedimentary deposits on the land, and a dead tree spread its spindly branches toward the sky. A heavy sulfur smell hung in the air.

This area was just as barren as his love life.

❧

That evening, Cheyenne sat on a split log with Arthur on her left and Noah on her right, and they watched the sparks of the campfire ascend into the evening sky. The group had left the geysers in the early afternoon and had spent an hour wading in Yellowstone Lake. After a picnic supper, Mr. Lindley and Derek built the campfire in a cleared space. Now the orphans and counselors sat around it.

Derek had taken a seat beside Arthur, along with his two charges, and Kandi was off to his left with her two girls.

Cheyenne looked down at Arthur, aware of Derek's presence on the other side. "I like how the sparks go up from the campfire. Do you see them?" She pointed above the fire, watching the little orange sparks ascend into the evening sky.

Arthur watched. "There's so many."

"That fire is hot. I wish we had some marshmallows to toast over the fire. Wouldn't that be good?"

"Yeah! Marshmallows!" Arthur's blue eyes lit up. "Why can't we have some, Anne?"

Derek turned to the boy. "Her name is Cheyenne, buddy."

"My name's not Buddy—it's Arthur."

Derek spread out his hands. "See there? You don't like it when you're called by the wrong name. It's the same way with Cheyenne."

Arthur gave her a puzzled glance before looking back at Derek. "But why is Anne so shy?"

Derek burst out laughing. "Oh, I get it!" He caught her eye. "Shy Anne!"

She laughed with him. "No one's ever called me *shy* before."

"Nope. This girl is not shy at all, Arthur." Derek continued laughing as he reached his hand over Arthur's head and grabbed her shoulder, pulling her toward him and bringing the three of them into an intimate circle.

Cheyenne's heartbeat pulsed into high gear, and she automatically placed her arm around his waist. Their hug only lasted a few seconds before Derek let go.

She glanced into his eyes, and he winked, causing her heart to race again.

Talk about sparks!

Arthur looked up at her, a puzzled expression on his sweet face. "What did he mean, Anne?"

She put her arm around him and gave him a hug. "Let me spell my name for you." Bending over, she found a short stick and carved out the letters in the dirt at their feet as Arthur watched. "That's how you spell Cheyenne. It's the same name as the capital city of Wyoming."

Derek leaned toward her to whisper in her ear. "He probably can't read."

She glanced into his eyes, and a little smile shadowed his face.

Mr. Lindley walked in front of the group and raised his voice. "We can't have a campfire without singing." He motioned toward a cowboy who had a guitar strapped around his back. "This is Jonas. He's going to lead us in some songs."

"Hello, ladies and gentlemen, boys and girls." Jonas had a deep voice that reminded Cheyenne of Rex.

Rex! She had completely forgotten about him. How could she do that? She certainly didn't want to cheat on him.

"Our first campfire song is an old classic—'Kumbaya.' Ya'll know that one? The words go: 'Kumbaya, my Lord, kumbaya. . .'"

Cheyenne raised her eyebrows. *That song was way before my time.* How would these kids know it? She looked over Arthur's head at Derek.

He rolled his eyes.

She grinned. Derek was just a good friend, right?

Too bad he was the one who made her heart zing.

sixteen

On Sunday morning, the orphans and volunteers filled the two vans and took off for a ranch located near Cody, Wyoming. Reaching their destination—a white farmhouse with a huge red barn—Derek helped Mr. Lindley herd everyone inside the barn. Bales of hay lined one side of the long, dusty room.

Mr. Lindley pointed. "Take a seat on the hay bales." He watched the children file by him. "Everyone sit down, please. Be sure you have your Bibles."

Other people from nearby ranches entered the building. The bale "seats" were soon filled to capacity.

Derek stood by the door, waiting for the children to settle down. Nathan and Joshua waited beside him. He placed his hand on Nathan's shoulder. "This is an authentic cowboy church, Nathan. What do you think about it?"

The boy looked around, an interested look in his eyes. "Cool."

Praise God! Derek had been praying for Nathan's attitude all weekend. "Let's sit back here, guys." He gestured toward the fourth row of bales since the first three were filled.

Nathan and Joshua sat down, and Derek settled next to them.

A moment later, Kandi plunked down beside him. "Is this where we're having church?" Frowning, she glanced around the barn.

Derek cut a glance toward her. *I cannot get rid of this girl.* "It's called a cowboy church." He raised his eyebrows. "Isn't it great?"

She lowered her voice. "But it's so. . .rustic."

"Take a deep breath, Kandi." He demonstrated, breathing

in the faint smell of manure. "The *pews* are here." He grinned.

She didn't even smile.

Cheyenne would have laughed her head off. "Uh, you need to sit with your girls." He motioned toward the first row where Cheyenne was sitting beside Madeline and Rayna.

Kandi grimaced but stood and walked to the front. She sat beside Rayna.

Derek released a sigh. *She is really getting on my nerves.*

❧

A half hour later, after several guitar-playing cowboys sang hymns with the congregation, one of the men opened his Bible. "My name is Pastor Wes. Let's look in God's Word this morning for a few minutes. God has a purpose, a will for your life. That's what we'll be talking about." He removed his cowboy hat. "But first, we'll begin our message with prayer."

Bowing his head, Derek prayed that the Lord would speak to his heart. He wanted to know God's will for his life.

Pastor Wes concluded his prayer and donned his hat. "If you have your Bible, open to Colossians chapter 1." He waited as the rustle of pages filled the room.

Derek pulled a New Testament from his shirt pocket. Beside him, Joshua and Nathan both opened their Bibles to Genesis and began to page through every book.

Leaning toward them, Derek whispered, "Let me help you." By the time he found Colossians in both Bibles, the pastor was reading verse 9.

" '. . .that ye might be filled with the knowledge of his will in all wisdom and spiritual understanding.' " Pastor Wes looked up. "God has a will, a purpose, for every Christian. If you have to struggle with what you feel is God's will in your life, then it might not be God's will." He paced the dusty floor in front of his congregation. "Before God calls you to do something, He will first give you the desire to do that very thing He wants you to do."

Derek stared at the pastor. *A desire.*

His eyes shifted to Cheyenne. He had a perfect view of her profile from where he sat. She kept her attention on the pastor, nodding her head slightly at what he was saying.

She is so pretty.

Another realization hit him. He couldn't go back to what he was before—a bachelor who didn't want to marry until age forty, or maybe never. He wanted what his brother had. He wanted a wife to love, children to raise for Christ's kingdom.

Did that involve Cheyenne?

It wouldn't be a *struggle* to have a relationship with her. His mind traveled back to that intimate moment in his truck, the time he held her in his arms at Tonya's party, the closeness at the campfire last night. He raised his eyebrows before a grin stole to his face.

No, it wouldn't be a struggle at all. Unless. . .

What if Rex wouldn't give her up without a fight? Or what if she really wanted to marry him?

Pastor Wes concluded his message. "Let's all stand for a closing prayer."

Derek stood as the congregation rustled to their feet. Bowing his head, he didn't hear the pastor's prayer. He had his own petition.

❧

Cheyenne was stuffed. The entire "church" had shared a huge dinner on the grounds, and now she sat on the grassy banks of the Shoshone River that ran through the rancher's property. The orphans played together, hiding behind the trees or wading in the river. She smiled at Arthur and Noah as they played near some large rocks at the river's edge.

"Be careful, boys," she called to them. "Don't fall in the water."

Arthur wielded a thin stick. "We're looking for snakes!"

"Yeah." Noah's thin face broke into a smile.

Cheyenne shook her head. *Boys will be boys.* "Don't let them bite you."

"We won't." Arthur turned back to a crevice between the rocks.

A few yards away, Derek stood on the river's bank, demonstrating how to skip stones across the water. A group of kids surrounded him, each one trying to ricochet a stone along the water's surface. Kandi stood by Derek's side.

Closing her eyes, the pastor's sermon entered her mind. Was Rex really God's will for her? Was she destined to get that inheritance, or would Mr. Sommers sink the money into his casino? How long before she would know?

A scripture verse penetrated her thoughts. *"Wait on the Lord: be of good courage, and he shall strengthen thine heart: wait, I say, on the Lord."*

Wait. Cheyenne would wait—for the Lord's plan, not her own. Strangely, she had more peace about adopting Arthur than she did about marrying Rex. If she legally adopted Arthur, that would take care of the child part, but she still needed a man.

A scream pierced the air.

Cheyenne's eyes flew open.

Noah ran toward her. "Miss Cheyenne!" His face was pale. "Arthur fell."

Cheyenne jumped up and followed him to the other side of the rocks. Arthur lay at the base of two large rocks, his right leg twisted at an odd angle. "Arthur!" Her heart pounding, she knelt beside him.

His blue eyes looked up into hers, his face wet with tears. "It hurts!"

"What happened?" Derek hunched down beside her.

"I don't know." Cheyenne clasped Arthur's hand as he whimpered.

"We were jumping on the rocks." Noah's voice quivered. "And Arthur fell."

"I'll take him to the house." Derek examined Arthur's leg before carefully lifting him.

Cheyenne stepped back, wiping a tear from her eye. *I should have been watching more closely!* All she could do now was pray.

❧

By the time Derek walked the five hundred feet to the house, the entire group of children and counselors followed en masse. Arthur cried softly in his arms, and Derek shifted him to a more comfortable position, trying to keep his voice calm. "You'll be okay, Arthur. You're very brave."

Mr. Lindley ran out of the house. "What happened?"

"We have a casualty." Derek nodded to Arthur's leg. "It might be broken."

"I'll take him to the hospital." Mr. Lindley looked at the crowd. "The rest of you get in the vans. It's time to go back to Casper anyway."

Amid a murmur of conversation, the counselors and children turned toward the vehicles.

"Mr. Lindley?" Holding Noah's hand, Cheyenne looked up at the orphanage director. "Could I go with Arthur? I feel so responsible."

Mr. Lindley shook his head. "These things happen, Cheyenne. It wasn't your fault. You need to go back with the others." He turned to Derek. "Take Arthur to Wesley's car." He nodded to a late-model Chevy on the driveway before striding toward the house. "I'll be right back."

Derek took a step to the car, but Cheyenne stopped him. She gazed at Arthur, who had stopped crying. His eyes were closed. She brushed back a lock of his blond hair. "I think he fainted, Derek."

"Looks like it." Derek kept his eyes on Cheyenne. If only he could pull her into his arms and comfort her. "Don't worry. He'll be okay."

"I hope so." She looked up, and her blue eyes held tears. "I wish I could stay with him." Looking down at Noah, she pulled on his hand. "Let's go, Noah." They slowly walked away.

Turning toward the Chevy, Derek bumped into Kandi who lingered by his side. A prick of annoyance hit him, and he used his head to motion to the van they came in. "Go with the others, Kandi."

A little pout formed over her lips before she left. Derek strode to the car, carrying Arthur in his arms.

"Derek." Mr. Lindley walked up with Pastor Wes. "Wesley will drive Arthur and me to the hospital. I'm putting you in charge of getting the orphans back to Casper. You'll have to take my place driving one of the vans."

"Okay."

Wes opened the back door of his car. "Lay him on the backseat." Derek did so, clicking a seat belt around the boy's middle. Pastor Wes got behind the wheel and started the engine.

Mr. Lindley walked around to the other side of the car. "Thanks, Derek. I called my wife, and she and the staff will be waiting for you when you arrive."

Derek nodded, relieved that his only responsibility would be driving the orphans back to the children's home.

❧

Two hours later they neared Casper, and Derek was thankful. The noise level from the nine orphans in the van had reached a peak when someone suggested they sing. With help from Jean and Leslie, the two counselors in the back, the van exploded with renditions of "Father Abraham" and "I'm in the Lord's Army."

At least they didn't sing "Kumbaya."

Kandi insisted on sitting in the front, replacing Nathan in the passenger seat. That annoyed Derek, but she didn't even attempt to talk to him. He spent the time praying for Arthur. Poor kid. Did he break anything besides his leg?

When the children finally expended their energy, the van became quiet. In the seat behind him, Cheyenne talked to Noah. Derek heard snatches of their conversation.

"Will Arthur be okay, Miss Cheyenne?"

"The Lord can make him better, Noah. We'll just have to pray and trust God."

Pray and trust God. That's what Derek would have to do concerning Cheyenne.

In the stillness a cell phone rang.

"That's mine." Kandi turned around to look back. "Cheyenne, could you get my purse?" She pointed. "It's under your seat."

"Here you go." Cheyenne handed it to her.

Pulling out her phone, Kandi flipped it open. "Hello?" She listened for a few moments then turned wide eyes on Derek. "Really? Oh that's terrible."

He frowned. "What happened?"

"My grandfather had a heart attack."

Derek raised his eyebrows. "Bruce?"

With a gasp, Cheyenne leaned toward Kandi. "Is he going to be all right?"

Kandi listened intently on the phone. "Yes, we're on our way to the Bolton Creek Children's Home. . . . I'll let you talk to Derek." She handed him the phone. "It's my dad. He wants to know how to get there."

Derek took the phone. After giving directions and then talking for several minutes, he closed the phone and handed it back to Kandi.

Cheyenne touched his shoulder. "Is Bruce going to be okay, Derek?"

"They don't know. He's at the county hospital in Lusk. Kandi's parents are driving in from Salt Lake City, and they're almost to Casper. We should get there about the same time that they arrive."

Kandi nodded. "I'll go with them to the hospital." Her eyes filled with tears. "What if Grandpa dies?"

Cheyenne reached out and touched Kandi's arm. "Let's pray for him." Without waiting for a response, she bowed her head. "Father in heaven, we lift Bruce up to You right now. Please heal him, Lord. Keep him on earth for a few more years. Comfort Kandi's parents, and keep them safe as they travel. And comfort Kandi, too. In Jesus' name, we ask. Amen."

"Amen!" Looking into the rearview mirror, Derek caught Cheyenne's eyes. "Thanks, Cheyenne."

"Yes, thank you." Kandi whispered the words before she turned back to the front.

Derek glanced at Kandi and saw her lower lip quiver. Without thinking, he grabbed her hand and squeezed it. "We'll trust the Lord. Your grandfather will pull through."

She just nodded.

He dropped her hand and concentrated on his driving. That was certainly nice of Cheyenne to pray for Kandi.

&

Cheyenne's heart dropped as she watched Derek squeeze Kandi's hand. *They certainly have a strange relationship.* Turning to the children sitting around her, she attempted to smile. "Let's sing another song."

Noah perked up. "Can we do the army song?"

"Yeah." Joshua smiled. "I like that one. Let's sing it loud."

Cheyenne glanced behind her at Jean and Leslie. "Are you guys going to join us?"

"Sure." Jean looked at the girls beside her and gave them a motherly smile. "We can sing loud, can't we?" She started the song, and everyone joined in, singing at the top of their lungs.

Within fifteen minutes, Derek parked the van in front of the orphanage. Cheyenne gazed up at the large house. She would pray about adopting Arthur someday. Maybe that was God's will for her.

seventeen

Cheyenne threw her duffel bag in the back of Derek's pickup, then opened the passenger door. Climbing in the cab, she pulled the door shut and rolled down the window. Kandi was still waiting for her parents, and Derek sat beside her on the front steps of the orphanage. The low murmur of his voice floated on the breeze. Kandi just sat there, staring at the ground.

Closing her eyes, Cheyenne leaned back against the seat, and Rex's face entered her mind. She would call him when she got home. At least he had a predictable, steady personality. Derek's behavior confused her. All weekend he had teased her and gazed into her eyes and often ignored Kandi. But since they received word about Bruce's heart attack, Derek showed a tender side toward her.

Derek had never seemed so unpredictable before.

A car drove up the driveway and stopped next to Derek's pickup. The car doors opened, and an overweight, bald man exited from the driver's side as a thin woman emerged from the passenger's side.

Kandi jumped up from the porch and ran to them. "Mom! Dad! I'm glad you're here!" While her parents hugged her, Derek slowly stood. Kandi turned to him. "This is Derek."

"Good to meet you." Mr. MacKinnon shook his hand.

"Oh Derek!" Mrs. MacKinnon threw her arms around his shoulders. "I'm so glad to meet you at last. Kandi's told us so much about you." She stepped back. "And look at you! Such a tall, handsome man! I can see why Kandi is totally smitten with you."

Derek's face colored slightly, but he smiled. "Thanks."

From her spot at the window, Cheyenne's lips parted. It

looked like Kandi's mother had already pegged Derek as her son-in-law.

Derek cleared his throat. "How is Bruce, by the way? Have you heard any further news?"

Kandi's dad opened his mouth, but her mom answered. "He's not out of the hospital yet, but they think he'll be all right. Agatha Collingsworth called us. I guess she's staying by his side, and we're so thankful for that."

Mr. MacKinnon turned to his wife. "We'd better get on our way."

"Yes, we need to go." Mrs. MacKinnon turned to Kandi. "Where's your suitcase, honey?"

While they got everything settled, Jean walked out the front door of the orphanage. "Derek?" She stopped in front of him. "Could you possibly drive me to Douglas? My husband's car won't start, so he can't pick me up."

"Sure, I can take you. It's right on the way." Derek motioned toward his truck. "I'm driving Cheyenne back to Fort Lob, but we have room for one more."

Cheyenne moved over to the middle of the seat. She wasn't sure if she was glad or disappointed that Jean would be going with them, then decided she was glad. At least she wouldn't have to talk to someone else's boyfriend all the way home.

❧

Derek tuned out the ladies' conversation. Cheyenne asked Jean a lot of questions, and Cheyenne got a lot of answers—the inside story about Jean's husband and teenaged kids. His mind drifted back to the MacKinnons. What had Kandi told her parents about him? Well, it didn't matter. When the MacKinnons went back to Salt Lake City, Kandi would forget all about him.

At least he hoped so.

Exiting the freeway, Derek drove his truck through the streets of Douglas as Jean gave him directions to her house. In another minute he was pulling into her driveway. He got out to retrieve her suitcase from the back.

" 'Bye, Jean!" Cheyenne leaned out the passenger window. "It was great to talk to you."

"Same here." Jean smiled as Derek set her suitcase down. "Thanks so much for the lift, Derek."

He nodded. "Anytime."

He climbed back in the cab, almost nervous that he and Cheyenne were finally alone. This ride back to Fort Lob could be a turning point in their relationship. Leaving the town of Douglas, he got back on the freeway.

Cheyenne leaned back against the seat, her eyes closed.

He glanced at her, and his heart stirred. "Tired?"

She opened her blue eyes and smiled at him. "A little." She sat up. "I'll be glad to get home. I'm going to call Rex and see how his weekend went."

Derek tightened his grip on the steering wheel. "So. . .you really like that old cowboy, huh?" *That was a stupid thing to say!*

Cheyenne's smile faded. "He's a very nice person, Derek, and a good Christian, too."

His cell phone chirped. *Saved by the bell!* He pulled it from his pocket and glanced at the number but didn't recognize it. He flipped the phone open and pulled it up to his face as he drove. "This is Derek."

"Hi, Derek." A loud male voice spoke in his ear. "Frank Lindley. I wanted to update you about Arthur."

"Oh good." Derek looked at Cheyenne. "It's Mr. Lindley. I'll put it on speakerphone so you can listen."

"Thanks." She leaned toward him.

Derek pressed a button and spoke into the phone. "How is he, Mr. Lindley?"

"It was a bad break, close to his knee. The doctor said he'll need to perform surgery and secure a pin to hold the bones in place."

Derek's pulse quickened. "Surgery? When are they doing that?"

"The hospital here in Cody is taking him to the Greenbrier Hospital in Casper. It's close to the orphanage. They'll move him tomorrow morning and then perform surgery on Tuesday or Wednesday." Mr. Lindley paused. "Arthur also has a slight concussion."

With a gasp, Cheyenne sat back. "A concussion?"

Derek spoke into the phone. "How bad is it?"

"I don't know, but they want to make sure that's cleared up before they do the surgery on his leg."

"I see." Derek glanced at Cheyenne. She turned away to the window, but not before he noticed a tear roll down her cheek. His heart clenched. "Thanks for the update, Mr. Lindley. We'll keep Arthur in prayer."

"I'll call later if there's any more news."

Derek bid him good-bye and cut off the call. He turned to Cheyenne. "I guess that's all we can do—pray."

"That's the best thing." She looked at him, her eyes bright with tears.

A strong urge to pull her into his arms and comfort her came over him. But he was driving, and besides, she belonged to Rex.

☙

Cheyenne smiled as Derek pulled into her driveway. "Thanks for the ride." She climbed out of the pickup's cab and shut the door; then waited as he grabbed her duffel bag from the back.

He handed it to her. "Here you go. And if Mr. Lindley calls about Arthur, I'll let you know."

"Thanks." She turned and trudged to the house. She needed to eat something. It was almost seven o'clock, and she hadn't eaten since they had lunch in Cody.

Stepping inside the house, she heard Derek's truck leave the driveway. She closed the door, and another sound penetrated her hearing. The television? Dad never watched TV.

She walked to the living room and stopped short. On the sofa, Dad sat beside Janet Oliver, his arm around her. She leaned her head on his shoulder.

Cheyenne's mouth dropped open. Taking a deep breath,

she stepped into the living room. "Hello."

Both turned to her, an identical look of surprise on their faces. Dad jumped up. "Hey, baby girl. How was Yellowstone? We didn't realize you were back."

We? Obviously Dad was not expecting her to arrive home this early.

Cheyenne forced a smile to her face. "It was great! Uh, but I'll tell you about it later. I'm kind of tired. Finish your movie." She turned and walked down the hallway.

In the safety of her bedroom, she closed the door and set down her duffel bag. *Wow! They sure looked cozy.* She plopped down on her bed.

Dad and Janet. Well, she was happy for them—two widowed people who had gone through tough times and deserved a "happily ever after" with each other.

From her purse, her cell phone rang. Sitting up, she glanced at the number before flipping open the phone. "Hi, Callie."

"You sound discouraged. Are you okay?"

A smile crept to Cheyenne's face. "You know me too well, girlfriend. Yeah, I'm discouraged. . .and tired. . .and hungry. Give me some good news. Please?"

"I do have good news. In fact, I have two pieces of good news."

"That's exactly what I need to hear." Cheyenne moved the pillow and sat back against the headboard. "I feel better already. What's the first thing?"

"The James Thomas Lob Museum is almost finished. Lane hopes to have the grand opening in October sometime."

"Oh Callie, that's wonderful." Cheyenne smiled, feeling her depression steal away. "Now you'll have the bookstore you always wanted. I know you're going to enjoy reading all those new books."

"I'm really looking forward to it. But we've been so busy, carting all that stuff over from the third floor of the library. Then it had to be cleaned and cataloged." She gave a little laugh. "Running the bookstore and souvenir shop will be easy compared to the last few months."

Cheyenne relaxed. "I can't wait to visit the museum."

"Hey, why don't you come out to the building site sometime? I'll show you around."

"I'll do that." Cheyenne tucked a strand of hair behind her ear. "Now what's the other good news you have for me?"

"Very few people know about this, so you're one of the first." Callie paused. "Lane and I are expecting a baby."

Cheyenne squealed. "Callie! Congratulations! When is the little bundle of joy due?"

"In April." Callie gave a happy sigh. "Do you realize that I met Lane just a year ago? And now we're married and we're going to have a child. Time goes by so fast."

"It does." Cheyenne brushed a tear from her eye. *That's exactly what I want!* "I'm so happy for you, Callie. That is just wonderful."

"God has been so good to us." A moment passed before Callie spoke again. "But I'm worried about you, Chey. Why are you so discouraged?"

She let a sigh escape her lips. "I don't know. It just seems that life is passing me by. Everything is working out for other people, but nothing is working out for me. I'm praying for the knowledge of God's will for my life, but I'm just not sure of anything."

"How are things with you and Rex? I thought you guys were really hitting it off."

"Oh, everything's fine with Rex, although. . ." Cheyenne rolled on her side. "Maybe I'm looking for the wrong things, but I don't think my feelings for him are as deep as they should be." She sighed. "And then this little boy I was supposed to be watching broke his leg. . . . It's a long story."

Callie paused. "That's too bad. I'll pray for the little boy. What's his name?"

"Arthur. He's five and so cute! A little roly-poly."

"Arthur," she repeated. "And listen, about Rex—the Lord

won't let you make a mistake. He might even be the one. I'll keep praying for you two."

Cheyenne sighed. "Thanks." *I think.*

eighteen

Derek rounded the corner in the Greenbrier Hospital corridor on Monday afternoon, looking for Room 116. His heart beat a little faster as he approached the door and pushed it open. Maybe he should have told the Lindleys he was coming instead of arriving unannounced.

Stepping into the room, he stopped short. Arthur lay on the hospital bed, hooked up to some machines, and sitting by his bedside was. . .

"Cheyenne?" Derek walked to the bed. "I didn't realize you were coming over here today."

A hint of surprise flitted across her face before she smiled. "Since I'm off work today, I thought I'd pay Arthur a visit."

He gazed at her pretty face. "We could have come together and saved some gas."

"Thanks, but my new Cavalier is working great." She turned to the little boy in the bed. "And you're doing great, aren't you, Arthur?"

"Yeah." Arthur's round face was pale, but he grinned. "I'm glad you came, Miss Anne."

Derek's lips twitched. "I hope you're not feeling too *shy*, Anne."

Cheyenne laughed. "I'm getting used to my new name, Mr. Derek." She nodded her head sideways toward Arthur. "But I don't think we can convince a certain someone that my name is actually C-h-e-y-e-n-n-e." Standing, she pulled another chair next to hers. "Have a seat."

"Thanks." Derek walked around the bed and sat down beside her.

"Look what Miss Anne brought me." Arthur held up a pack of crayons with a long, thin coloring book. A cartoon character grinned from the cover.

"Cool." Derek smiled at him. "How are you feeling, Arthur?"

"Okay." Arthur thumbed through the book.

"He's on a lot of pain medicine." Cheyenne lowered her voice. "The concussion is gone, so the doctor wants to do surgery tomorrow morning."

Derek leaned toward her, relishing their closeness. "I'm surprised the Lindleys aren't here."

"Mrs. Lindley stayed by Arthur's bedside all night." Cheyenne tucked a strand of hair behind her ear. "I told her to go home and get some rest. I'm staying with Arthur until she gets back."

Derek raised his eyebrows. *Talk about a servant's heart.* "Want some company, Cheyenne? I'll stay with you until Mrs. Lindley returns."

"That would be. . .nice. Thanks, Derek." Cheyenne turned back to Arthur, who was leaning on his pillows, a listless look on his face. She walked to his side and smoothed his blond hair back from his forehead. "You need to sleep, honey. Mr. Derek and I will be right here if you need us. Okay?"

Arthur nodded before closing his eyes.

Cheyenne looked at Derek. "Let's sit over there." She pointed to some vinyl-covered chairs by the wall. "We can talk, and we won't bother him."

Derek stood and waited for Cheyenne to sit down before he took a seat beside her. He looked forward to being with her for a while.

His cell rang, and he glanced at the number. "Sorry, Cheyenne. I'll be right back." He stood and headed for the door. "Hello, Kandi."

"Hi, Derek. How are you?" She sounded a little breathless.

"Good." He pulled the door closed behind him and walked down to the end of the hospital corridor. "I heard that Bruce is recovering now, and your family left this morning for Salt Lake City. You made it back okay?"

"Yes."

He waited a beat, knowing she wouldn't expand that one word into an explanation. But he wasn't about to carry the conversation. "Why did you call?"

"Well. . .I haven't heard from you, and. . .I just thought I'd call. To talk."

He smirked. Kandi talking in a phone conversation? "Okay. What do you want to talk about?"

"I—I want to keep our. . .relationship going, you know? We need to call each other every day or e-mail."

With a sigh, he looked out the window at the end of the hallway, viewing the hospital parking lot. *Lord, help me here!* He didn't want to hurt her feelings. "Um. . .a long-distance relationship usually doesn't work out, Kandi."

"We can make it work. I have Skype on my laptop. We could see each other every evening and get to know one another."

He shook his head. "I've been praying a lot about my future, trying to discern God's will for my life, and I feel—"

"There's another girl."

Derek's lips parted as Cheyenne's pretty face popped into his mind. "Uh, yeah." It was true, wasn't it? "There is another girl I'm interested in."

"I knew it." Kandi sounded grim. "I knew you were involved with someone else. You were so mean to me at Yellowstone, and I went just because of you!"

He raised his eyebrows. "I didn't ask you to go."

"Well, I thought you wanted to spend time with me. I was enjoying our relationship, and all of a sudden you changed. Now you like Cheyenne."

His eyebrows shot up. Was it that obvious? "We're good friends—"

"I saw the way you looked at her. Why were you leading me on?"

"I wasn't leading you on."

"Were you just using me to make her jealous? Obviously

you're in love with her."

In love? "No, Kandi—"

"I don't want to talk to you again."

He breathed out a relieved sigh. "Okay, if that's the way you feel."

A faint *click* followed.

"Kandi? Are you still there?" When she didn't answer, Derek closed his phone. *Strange conversation!* But he was glad Kandi had ended their "relationship." Glancing out the window at the blue sky, he spent a few moments in prayer. Was he in love with Cheyenne? Slowly he walked back down the hallway.

Pushing open the door to Arthur's room, he heard a soft feminine voice as he stepped inside. Mrs. Lindley sat beside Cheyenne on the vinyl chairs. Both women's heads were bowed, their hands clasped together, as the older woman prayed.

". . .and we not only pray for Arthur, Father, but for Cheyenne here as well."

Derek stayed near the door, bowing his head as he listened.

"She has expressed an interest in adopting Arthur someday, Lord, and we would love to see her become his mother. But she needs a husband. I pray that You might provide, as You have promised."

Derek's eyes opened. *Should I be standing here?*

"She has someone in mind, Father, but she's not sure if he would welcome Arthur into their home." Mrs. Lindley hesitated. "You know who he is, Father. Speak to his heart. . . ."

Derek stepped back into the corridor. *"She has someone in mind."* Rex Pierson, of course.

He frowned. *I would welcome Arthur into our home.* If he were married to Cheyenne, Derek would be more than happy to adopt Arthur and raise him as the next generation for the Lord. But it looked like Cheyenne wanted Rex for that job.

Derek clenched his jaw. He was going to end up as an old bachelor.

ᴕ

The next Sunday after the first hymn, Cheyenne started to replace the hymnbook in the pew rack in front of her, but Rex's knobby fingers reached out.

"Allow me," he whispered as he grabbed the book.

"Thanks." She smiled at him.

He returned her smile with a wink before placing his arm on the pew behind her. Cheyenne leaned toward him. If only she loved him! She had a sinking feeling that she never would.

Pastor Reilly began making the announcements. "Don't forget about our Sweet Memories banquet this Friday night. We'll have a potluck dinner, so you ladies need to bring your favorite dish."

Cheyenne tucked a strand of hair behind her ear. Now was not the time to dwell on her problems. What should she make for the banquet? Maybe she could debut the new enchilada recipe she had invented, inspired by an assortment of damaged cans and boxes from her dad's store. She had volunteered to help serve coffee and punch at the banquet and help with the cleanup afterward.

"After the dinner," Pastor Reilly continued, "we'll have a PowerPoint presentation from the past forty years. Forty years of ministry in this church for the wife and me." He smiled. "And I expect to be your pastor for the next forty."

Everyone chuckled. In forty years, Pastor Reilly would be more than a hundred years old.

Cheyenne looked at Rex and grinned. "He just might make it," she whispered.

ᴕ

On Monday Cheyenne parked her Cavalier in front of the orphanage in Casper. She patted the dashboard before she got out. *Thank You, Lord, for this car.* It was great not to worry about an old car breaking down. She should have replaced the Dart months ago when it started falling apart.

It had been a week since she'd seen Arthur in the

hospital—too long for her. If only it wasn't such a long drive to Casper. Now he was recovering at the children's home, and his leg was in a cast. She thought of Mrs. Lindley's prayer from last week. Would she ever be Arthur's mom?

As she walked up the front steps, the door opened and Mr. Lindley stepped outside.

"Cheyenne! I suppose you're here to visit Arthur?"

She nodded. "Is that okay?"

"More than okay—it's great!" His dark eyes twinkled. "I think Arthur views you as his surrogate mother already."

"Really?" She dropped her voice. "Have you told him I want to adopt him?"

"No, of course not. My wife and I are keeping that secret to ourselves—and praying about it, too." He grinned. "The Lord has a plan."

"I've been wondering about Arthur's background. I was going to ask your wife about it last week, but I didn't have the chance. Has he been living here a long time?"

Mr. Lindley shook his head. "His mom just died four months ago from a blood clot. She was a single mother—never married as far as I know. But she was a Christian and attended our church."

Cheyenne raised her eyebrows. "So you knew Arthur? When his mom died, I suppose you offered to take him in."

"Actually, she had listed the children's home in her will." He folded his arms. "If anything happened to her, she wanted the home to take care of her son, with the request to find a Christian couple to adopt him."

Cheyenne's heart picked up its beat. "That was in her will?" She shook her head. "Unbelievable."

"The Lord is working in that boy's life." Mr. Lindley smiled. "We'll take good care of Arthur for you, Cheyenne." He walked down the steps. "Maybe someday, when you marry. . ."

She sighed. *Yeah, maybe someday.*

છે

On Thursday Cheyenne relaxed on a chair at The Beauty

Spot as Tonya cut her hair. She would be glad when her hair was back to shoulder length with the split ends cut off.

"Bruce is finally getting out of the hospital tomorrow." With a broom, Aggie swept some hair into a dustpan from another customer. "His son's wife calls us every day. I really like them, and of course Kandi is so cute. She's just the sweetest thing."

Closing her eyes, Cheyenne let a small sigh escape. *Kandi again.* She remembered Derek getting a phone call from Kandi at the hospital. Since that day, Cheyenne had not seen much of him.

Tonya sectioned off a strand of hair and pinned it to the top of Cheyenne's head. "You won't be working tomorrow, will you, Aggie?"

"Nope." Aggie put the broom in the closet. "I'm driving Bruce home from the hospital in the morning, and I'm going to pamper him all day."

"Is your famous fried chicken on the menu for supper?"

"Are you joking?" Aggie sat down on the other beautician chair. "The doc gave me a list of foods Bruce can't eat, and fried chicken is right at the top. It's going to be spinach and fish for the next few months." She gave a little laugh. "But it will be the most delicious spinach and fish he's ever had." Aggie touched the yellow butterfly barrette in her hair. "I'm not working for the rest of the week, but Connie will be here to help you out, Tonya. And don't call me. I'll be taking care of my man—cooking and cleaning."

"You'll be like a regular wife to him." Tonya grinned.

"A wife?" Aggie grunted. "More like a housekeeper. I'll just be the servant girl. Bruce will never see me as wife material." She pursed her pink lips. "Don't know why, but I just can't please that man. I still don't see anything wrong with that tangerine lipstick. Always liked the orange color myself, but Bruce is more comfortable with my makeup toned down." She sighed.

Tonya picked up a comb from the counter. "I'm thankful

Murray loves me the way I am. He's so sweet."

"But did ya'll notice what happened?" Aggie frowned at Tonya. "You and Murray are the ones who got Bruce and me together in the first place, and then you two up and marry while we're still floundering in friendship." She turned her frown on Cheyenne. "Now isn't that just the way it goes? Bruce will never propose to me. It's like I told Murray that day he came in to get his hair cut—Bruce and I will be friends forever, and only friends, if someone don't nudge that man toward me. And even after I asked Murray to put a bug in his ear—"

"Aggie!" Tonya cocked an eyebrow at her. "That was my idea, and Murray and I had to push you into it."

"But it did no good! All those changes I made for Bruce, and we're still only friends. It will be unrequited love for the rest of my days."

Unrequited love. Derek's face popped into Cheyenne's mind. She had loved him for all those years. "I know how you feel." As soon as the words left her mouth, she regretted saying them.

Aggie leaned toward her, interest sparking in her dark eyes. "I've seen you with that handsome Rex Pierson. I bet you have a case on him!"

Cheyenne smiled. "We have a date tonight at the Four Seasons."

"Ooh!" Tonya snipped at a section of hair with professional panache. "That's exciting, Cheyenne. I hope you guys have a great time."

"Thanks." If only the Lord would answer her prayers. Something had to change tonight in their relationship.

❧

Walking into the kitchen, Derek answered the phone on the fifth ring. "Derek here."

"It's about time you picked up the receiver, son."

He grinned. "Hi, Mom! How are the RV travelers?"

"Oh I love traveling and seeing the beauty of God's

creation. Right now we're staying at The Lakes in Kentucky. This is a beautiful area. So many trees, so much water. . ."

"You sound like a travel brochure."

She laughed. "I can't believe we won't be home for a couple of months. I'm taking notes on all the places we're visiting, and we've met so many interesting people." She paused. "Now Derek, you're keeping the dishes washed up, aren't you?"

"Uh, sure." He eyed the stack of dirty plates and bowls in the sink. *I need to buy some paper plates!* "Don't worry, Mom, you'll come back to a clean house."

"You need to keep up with it, Derek. Be sure to dust and vacuum every week."

He rolled his eyes. "Yes, ma'am."

"How is everything going on the ranch?"

He glanced out the kitchen window and caught sight of Hector's overalls as he disappeared into the barn. "Good. Miguel and Hector are helping run everything, but we haven't had any problems. No wolves. No coyotes." He shrugged even though Mom couldn't see him over the phone.

"That's good. I know you're taking good care of those sheep. Don't forget to watch out for my favorite little lamb."

"Snowflake?" He grinned, remembering how Mom had bottle-fed the tiny lamb, turning her into a pet. "She's a happy camper, Mom. Just like you. I think Snowflake knows she's not destined for the slaughterhouse this fall."

Mom laughed. "None of the lambs know that, but Snowflake is going to be a big fluffy ewe someday." The sound of static filled the phone. "I need to go, son. This cell phone needs to be recharged. We love you, Derek."

"Love you, too, Mom."

Hanging up the phone, he gazed out the kitchen window. He could barely see the flock of sheep resting on a hillside. *I should go out there and see how Shep is doing.*

As he opened the back door, a feeling of loneliness

overwhelmed him. He missed Mom and Dad being here.
There was no one to talk to in this big old house.

Maybe staying single was not such a good idea.

nineteen

That evening, Cheyenne folded her napkin next to her plate and looked across the table at Rex. He was dressed up for this date, wearing a dress shirt with a Western tie and black jeans. And he had actually shaved.

"Should we order some coffee, darlin'?"

"That would be nice, Rex."

He signaled the waiter. "Two coffees. And please bring a lot of creamers for the little lady."

She raised an eyebrow. "The 'little lady,' Rex? I've never considered myself little."

Reaching across the table, he took her hands in his work-worn ones. "You are one pretty lady, Cheyenne, and you're pretty special to me."

The waiter set two cups and saucers on the table then poured steaming black coffee from a silver urn. He set the pot down along with a small pitcher of cream.

She smiled at the man. "Thank you."

Rex let go of her hands, and she poured cream into her cup. As she stirred her coffee, she thought of how romantic this evening should be—a handsome cowboy, a gourmet dinner, a perfect atmosphere.

And I feel nothing.

They sipped their coffee for a few moments, and then Rex set down his cup and once again took her hands in his. He cleared his throat.

"There's something I've been meanin' to ask you." His brown eyes held hers. "Would you do me the honor of becoming Mrs. Pierson?"

Cheyenne drew in a sharp breath. *He's proposing?*

Rex tightened his grip. "I would provide well for you,

darlin'. Even that little bungalow feels lonesome. It's too big for just me. We could have a passel of kiddos someday or even adopt that little boy you like."

Cheyenne's mind raced. Wasn't this what she had been praying for? She could get married and adopt Arthur in time to fulfill all the stipulations of her grandmother's will.

Lord, is this what You want for me?

She looked across the table into Rex's eyes and knew what her answer had to be.

Taking a deep breath, she looked down at their hands. "I've really enjoyed getting to know you these last few weeks, Rex, but I can't marry you." She glanced up at him. "You are a wonderful man, and you deserve a woman who really loves you." She paused. "I'm not that woman."

Rex let go of her hands and leaned back in his chair.

Tears crept to her eyes. "I'm sorry."

He sighed. "If that's the way you feel, then we'll part as friends."

Relief flooded through her. "Thank you, Rex." She now had no prospects for a husband, she might not get to adopt Arthur, and she probably wouldn't inherit Grandmother's millions, but the decision was made.

And she knew it was the right one.

❧

Derek was late.

On Friday night he entered the fellowship room in the basement of the church for the Sweet Memories banquet, hoping he could find a seat. Long tables stretched the length of the room, and all the seats were filled with talking, eating people.

As his eyes swept the room, he noticed Janet Oliver sitting next to Jim Wilkins. Derek raised his eyebrows. *Interesting.* Jim and Janet had been sitting together in church last Sunday, too.

Next to Janet, Aggie and Bruce sat side by side. Bruce had been out of the hospital for a few days, and he seemed to be doing well. Derek was glad Kandi was back with her family. Their relationship had been a good learning experience, as his mother would say.

What he learned was that he needed to stay away from quiet, possessive girls.

With a coffeepot in her hand, Cheyenne walked up to him, sporting a jean jacket and a long pink skirt. "Hi, Derek! Did you just arrive?" Her blue eyes gazed up into his as she smiled.

What a knockout! "I like your haircut—and your outfit, too."

"Thanks! Tonya did my hair, and this was my favorite outfit in high school. I thought it would be appropriate for the Sweet Memories banquet." She grinned. "I can't believe I fit into it after ten years!"

He returned her grin, enjoying her bubbly personality. This was the girl he loved to be around. "You look really pretty tonight."

A look of surprise skittered across her face, and their eyes locked. Derek was a little surprised himself that he had blurted out his thoughts.

Someone called Cheyenne's name, and they both turned to look at a nearby table. A man raised his coffee cup. "Refill?" he asked.

"I'll be right there." She turned back to Derek and motioned toward a long table of food by the wall. "Help yourself to the food. I'll find a chair for you."

"Thanks." His eyes followed her as she walked away. Then he looked around. Where was Rex?

He passed his sister Callie, who was filling water glasses.

Walking to the table, he picked up a paper plate and dished a spoonful of green bean casserole on his plate. *Why am I so hung up on Cheyenne?* He added a chicken leg. *Does the Lord really want me to stay single?* The scalloped potato dish was almost empty, but he scraped out a spoonful. *What do I really want?* He threw a dollop of baked beans on his plate. *Even if I want Cheyenne, will she want me?* Glancing at the scanty dessert section, he added two squares of cake to his plate. *I might not have the chance to find out.*

Turning from the table, he glanced around. Cheyenne motioned to him from the end of the room. He made his way toward the back, greeting several people on the way.

"You can sit here, Derek." Cheyenne laid her hand on a folding chair at the end of one of the long tables.

"Thank you." Derek took the seat.

"You're welcome." She glanced at his plate. "You didn't get any of my enchiladas."

He looked at the food on his plate. "Did I miss something?"

She smiled. "I'll get some for you."

As Cheyenne left, Derek greeted the Newmans, the young couple on his right. They had two children who kept their attention, so they didn't say much.

Edna Beazer sat on his left. She leaned toward him and smiled, showing off her straight white dentures. "Derek Brandt! I haven't seen you for ages."

He glanced at the older woman as he dug the plastic fork into his food. Her thin hair was tinted blue. "How are you doing, Mrs. Beazer?"

"Oh, my arthritis is acting up something fierce, but besides that, I'm better than middling."

A drop of her spit landed on the table, and Derek deftly moved his plate to the right.

Cheyenne came back and set a small plate beside his arm. "They were almost gone. Here's the last of it. This recipe is making its debut tonight since I made it up."

"Thanks." Derek glanced at the small square of layered tortillas, meat, and cheese. "Looks good." He pulled the plate toward him and took a bite.

Mrs. Beazer looked up at Cheyenne. "What are you calling the new recipe, dear?"

Cheyenne shrugged. "Ten-Layer Enchiladas."

"Wow, this is really good, Cheyenne." Derek took another bite.

"Glad you like it." With a smile, Cheyenne picked up a coffeepot from the table and moved away, refilling cups.

"Where are your parents, Derek?" Mrs. Beazer sucked in her dentures. "I didn't see them Wednesday night in church, and they aren't here tonight."

"Mom and Dad are traveling. They purchased an RV and left town on Monday. They're planning to travel around the southern states during the next few months."

Edna's thin eyebrows raised. "So you're all alone in that big old house of yours?"

Nodding, Derek swallowed another bite of enchiladas. "Until November. They plan to be home for the holidays."

She placed a bony hand on his arm. "You must be lonely."

"I'm doing fine by myself, thanks." He wasn't about to let Mrs. Beazer or anyone else know how lonely he really was. He finished eating and headed for the nearest trash can to throw away his plate. Callie struggled to pull a full trash bag out of the can.

"Hey, let me help you do that."

"Oh thanks, Derek." Callie stood back as he took over. "You wouldn't believe how intense smells can be when you're pregnant."

He quirked an eyebrow at her. "I've never been pregnant, so I'll take your word for it."

She laughed. "Just put the full bag by the back door. I'm going to sit with Lane."

"Hey, Callie."

She turned back to him.

He lowered his voice. "I noticed Rex Pierson isn't here. I thought Cheyenne would be sitting with him."

"Didn't you hear?" Callie's eyes widened. "They broke up."

He stared at her. "What?"

"Yes." She glanced around before moving closer to him. "Rex proposed to Cheyenne last night, and she turned him down."

The pastor walked to the front of the room and stood

behind a small lectern.

"We'd better take our seats," Callie whispered.

"Welcome to our Sweet Memories banquet." Pastor Reilly glanced around the tables. "Most of you are finished, so we'll begin our program."

His head still spinning, Derek reclaimed his seat. *Cheyenne is available!* He couldn't believe it. This changed everything.

As the pastor spoke about the history of the church, several ladies who had helped in the kitchen took seats with their families. Cheyenne came out from the kitchen also, but she didn't sit down. Clasping her hands in front of her, she stood by the wall near the food table.

The pastor motioned behind him to a large white screen. "Since a picture is worth a thousand words, we have a PowerPoint that Ralph Little put together. These are slides from the last forty years—from the very first year my wife and I came to Fort Lob until the present." He smiled. "But first we'll listen to a number from our own men's quartet—The Four Methuselahs."

Derek folded his arms on the table. He loved to hear the "Methuselahs" sing. All four men were over sixty years old, but they harmonized perfectly.

The men walked to the front, all sporting minty-green blazers with yellow handkerchiefs in the front pocket. A quiet hum was heard, and then the men broke out into a rousing a cappella rendition of "Joshua Fit de Battle of Jericho." When they finished, Derek joined in the applause.

"Thank you, men." The pastor moved the lectern to one side. "If someone douses the lights, we'll watch our PowerPoint presentation."

The pastor took a seat in the front, and the lights went out. Derek glanced over at Cheyenne, whom he could barely see. Was she going to stand during the entire program?

I am going to take care of that girl.

Grabbing his chair, Derek walked to where she stood. "Cheyenne." He kept his voice low as the presentation started with music. "Here's a chair." He unfolded it next to her.

She glanced down. "But that's your chair," she whispered.

"No, it's yours." He motioned toward it. "Sit."

She smiled as she took a seat. "Thanks, Derek."

Folding his arms, he leaned against the wall next to her. The room was quiet as the photos faded in and out with the music. The first pictures were before Derek's time, although he saw photos of his parents as young people. Aggie, Bruce MacKinnon with his first wife, Edna Beazer and her husband, Fred and Janet Oliver. . . All were captured in the prime of life. As the years moved along, Derek began to appear as a little kid with his brother and sisters.

At one picture, Cheyenne turned and looked up at him with a smile. "Remember that?" she whispered.

A group of elementary children smiled for the camera. As a ten-year-old boy, Derek stood next to Cheyenne and Callie, who were both eleven. All three of them held up colorful award ribbons.

Derek hunkered down next to Cheyenne's chair. "Neighborhood Bible Time, wasn't it?"

"Yes." She grinned. "I loved that summer. We had so much fun." She turned her attention back to the slides.

Cheyenne had always loved fun, and Derek had always loved being around her, even when they were kids.

He glanced at her profile. Could they have a future together?

At the end of the PowerPoint, Derek stood and leaned against the wall.

Pastor Reilly came back to stand behind the lectern. "You have just witnessed the last forty years of this church's history. The Lord has been so good to us, faithfully guiding us, leading us to people who need Him, and strengthening our members in the faith." He motioned toward the front table. "But I couldn't have accomplished the work of this ministry without my dear wife by my side. We have served the Lord together all these years. She's been such a blessing to me." He turned to her. "Honey, stand up."

Someone started clapping, and the audience joined in. Mrs. Reilly smiled at her husband and then at the church people.

Derek didn't clap. He stared at the Reillys. *"We have served the Lord together."* Tonya's voice flitted through his mind. *"That's crazy. He doesn't have to remain single to serve the Lord."*

He glanced at Cheyenne. He knew that she cared about him. She even cared about his sheep. Maybe she even loved him.

And I love her! Kandi had been right about that.

The pastor was winding down his comments. "Thank you for attending this banquet. It has certainly been sweet memories for my wife and myself. Now let's close—"

"Pastor?" Bruce MacKinnon stood. "Before we dismiss, could I give a short testimony?"

The pastor nodded. "Certainly, Bruce. Go right ahead."

Bruce swung around to face most of the crowd. "You all know that I had a heart attack almost two weeks ago. Being confined to the hospital, flat on my back for a week, I had a lot of time to think about my life. I'm so thankful God spared me, and I want to use my remaining years to serve Him." He glanced down at Aggie who smiled up at him. "I also realize that life is short. Therefore in front of all my friends, I'd like to ask you, Agatha Collingsworth, to marry me."

Aggie's mouth dropped open, and several gasps could be heard around the room.

But Aggie recovered quickly. Pushing back her chair, she jumped up to stand beside him. "Why Bruce, you old codger, you! In front of all these people, I can't say *no*!"

Everyone laughed as Bruce drew her into his arms and hugged her.

Pastor Reilly raised his voice. "Congratulations to the happy couple! You are all dismissed."

Chairs scraped against the tile floor as everyone stood, and the noise level grew to a joyous din. Derek wanted to talk to Cheyenne, but she rushed off to join the crowd of well-wishers surrounding Bruce and Aggie.

Perhaps now was not the time to talk to Cheyenne.

Life is short. Derek turned and walked out the door to the parking lot. He would go home and spend the next hour on his knees, praying that someday his house would be filled with his wife's laughter and the happy voices of their children.

twenty

On Saturday Cheyenne hooked the leash to Marshal's collar. "Okay, Marsh, we're ready to go." Opening the door, she walked out into the early evening.

I'm not jogging! She would take an easy-paced walk and pray. She hadn't even donned her sweats, opting instead for jeans and a blue T-shirt.

It had been raining that afternoon when she got home from work, and now a fresh scent hung in the air. She took a deep breath as she walked down the sidewalk with Marshal by her side.

Life is short. That's what Bruce had said last night at the Sweet Memories banquet. Cheyenne couldn't believe he asked Aggie to marry him in front of everyone! Of course Aggie loved the attention, and she finally got what she wanted—the promise of marriage to Bruce MacKinnon. Cheyenne was so happy for her.

And I'm happy that I'm not going to marry Rex.

A horn honked, making her jump. She glanced at the Town Car driving by and waved at her dad. He was coming home from work.

Crossing the street, she made her way toward the park. Walking Marshal had become an everyday habit for her. Since her birthday, she had lost nineteen pounds. She even had to buy some new clothes. But the best thing about going to the park was the time she spent in prayer as she walked.

She couldn't imagine any man more perfect for her than Derek Brandt. But maybe the Lord had other plans. She sighed.

It was sad that a casino owner would be getting all of Grandmother's money.

Derek lifted his truck keys from the hook by the door. For a moment, his heart beat a hard staccato, and he almost put the keys back. But after spending time in prayer last night, he knew Cheyenne was God's will for him.

"Don't be a coward!" he admonished himself.

Leaving the ranch, he drove the seven miles to Fort Lob. It only took a few turns from Main Street to arrive at Cheyenne's house. He drove up the driveway and parked behind Jim's Town Car. His hands shook slightly as he climbed out of the truck and approached her house.

He couldn't believe he was so nervous. *This is Cheyenne, for goodness' sake.* Taking a deep breath, he knocked on the door.

A moment later the door opened, but it wasn't Cheyenne.

"Hi, Derek!" Jim boomed out. "What can I do for you?"

"Is Cheyenne here?"

"No, she's on a walk with Marshal. I passed her on my way home. She probably went to the park."

"Oh." A sense of relief spread through him, yet at the same time, Derek knew exactly what his next step should be. "Uh, could I come in and talk to you a minute?" He didn't want to talk at the door. With Jim's loud voice, the whole neighborhood would hear their conversation.

Jim stepped back. "Sure. Come on in."

"Thanks." Derek followed him inside to the living room.

"Have a seat." Jim motioned to the sofa. "Can I get you something to drink?"

Derek shook his head. "I just have a question to ask you."

Jim took a seat across from him in a La-Z-Boy recliner, and his blue eyes—the exact color as Cheyenne's—stared at him. "So what's the problem?"

"It's not really a problem." Derek tapped his fingers on the arm of the sofa. Where should he start? "Well. . .I've loved your daughter for a long time." *Whoa!* He couldn't believe those were the first words out of his mouth.

A look of surprise passed over Jim's face, but then he

smiled. "I'm glad to hear that, Derek. Cheyenne thought you weren't interested in her. I understand you were dating someone else?"

"Kandi MacKinnon, but she's out of the picture now, and I hear that Cheyenne is not dating Rex anymore."

"That's true." A hint of a smile touched Jim's lips.

With a kick of determination, his nervousness vanished. He would tell Jim the truth. "I wish I had started dating Cheyenne years ago, but I thought the Lord wanted me to remain single to serve Him. But then at the banquet last night, Pastor Reilly said he couldn't have accomplished the work of his ministry without his wife. They served the Lord together all their lives." Derek spread out his hands. "Something hit me. I realized I've loved Cheyenne—for years. The Lord showed me that if I want to serve Him, I need a wife by my side." A little warmth crept up his neck. "Does that make sense? Cheyenne has a servant's heart, and she's a lot of fun, and she's pretty, and. . .and I love her."

Jim raised his eyebrows. "Uh, so, are you asking for her hand in marriage?"

"Yes!" Derek nodded. Didn't he make that clear? "Sorry. I don't do well at explaining things, but I do want your permission and your blessing to marry your daughter—if she'll have me."

"I'm more than happy to give my blessing to your marriage. In fact, this is an answer to prayer—not only my prayers, but Cheyenne's mom's prayers as well. As far as Cheyenne's answer. . ." He shrugged. "All you can do is ask." Then he grinned. "But I doubt that she'll turn you down."

"That's good." Derek got to his feet. "Thanks, Jim. I'll drive over to the park and see if I can find her."

Jim stood and thrust out his hand. "Welcome to the family, son."

With a laugh, Derek shook it. "Aren't you being a little premature? Cheyenne hasn't agreed to marry me yet."

"She will." Jim's smile faded. "Oh wait a minute. Before you leave, I want to give you something."

❧

Cheyenne took a seat on a park bench—the same bench next to the lamppost where she and Dad had their discussion several weeks ago. "Let's rest awhile, Marsh. I can see you're tired."

Marshal sat down on his haunches and panted.

The twilight deepened, and the light above her turned on. Two boys whizzed by on their bikes. Then all was quiet. Taking a deep breath of warm summer air, she rubbed Marshal's ear.

"It's just you and me, boy." Her thoughts drifted back to last night at the banquet when Derek had given her his chair. *That was so sweet of him.*

Closing her eyes, she felt a tear creep out from her lashes. *Why am I crying?* Pulling a tissue from her jeans pocket, she wiped the tear away. *I will wait, Lord.* Once again, she closed her eyes and breathed in the warm air, spending several minutes in prayer.

Someone sat down on the bench beside her. "Cheyenne?"

Her eyes flew open. Derek gazed at her from under the brim of his cowboy hat. He wore a Western shirt, and his long legs were clad in jeans.

"Hi." He smiled at her. "Glad I found you."

Her heart leaped. "Um, hi!" What was he doing here? He had such a strange look on his face. "Do you need something?"

"Well. . .I went to your house, but your dad told me you were walking the dog. He figured you were at the park."

She shrugged. "Here I am."

Derek removed his cowboy hat and held it in his hands a moment before setting it on the bench. He cleared his throat. "I've been thinking a lot about my life lately—you know, relationships and stuff."

She frowned. "Relationships?"

He met her eyes. "I learned a few things, Cheyenne. In fact, I learned a lot through dating Kandi—a real trial-and-error relationship."

She stiffened. Why was he talking about this? She didn't want to hear about his relationship with Kandi. What did he want? Advice?

He cleared his throat. "I really don't have much experience in relationships."

That's obvious! She sniffed. "I'm sure you and Kandi will be very happy—"

"Kandi?" He placed his arm on the back of the bench. "Is that what you think? I'm planning to marry her?"

She frowned. "It sure looked that way at Yellowstone. The two of you were together every second. And then her mom said—" *Oh! I'm really putting my foot in my mouth!* "Never mind." She looked away.

"Cheyenne." Derek gently placed his fingers on her chin and pulled her face toward him. "I had nothing to do with that closeness at Yellowstone. Kandi is a very possessive person, I found out." He dropped his hand but looked deeply into her eyes. "I learned two things through my short relationship with Kandi."

She gazed up into his eyes, trying to blink away the tears that insisted on appearing.

Derek curved his arm around her shoulders. "I learned that God does not want me to remain single in order to serve Him, and I learned that. . ." His gaze dropped to her lips before it came back to her eyes. "I love you, and I've loved you for a long time."

Cheyenne's head spun. "Me? You—you love *me*? Not Kandi?" Was that what he'd been trying to tell her with all his talking in circles?

A smile flitted across his lips. "Yes, you, Cheyenne. There's never been anyone else. No one but you."

Her lips parted. Was this really happening? Was she actually sitting on a park bench on a warm summer night with Derek Brandt? Had he just said that he loved her? The moment seemed surreal as she gazed into his eyes.

But in the next moment, her senses flooded back. God was answering all her prayers in a single moment of time!

"Oh Derek," she whispered. "I love you, too."

He lowered his head, and her hands seemed to slide around his neck of their own accord. His arms tightened around her as his lips touched hers.

That same surreal feeling flew through Cheyenne as Derek kissed her, but at the same time, she felt an aura of peace. God's peace.

This is where I belong.

In another moment Derek raised his head. He gave her a little half smile then leaned in to kiss her again. Cheyenne didn't mind. This time she kissed him back with all the passion she'd been saving up for him.

Finally he sat back. "Wow, Cheyenne. If I had known you kiss like that. . ." He waggled his eyebrows.

She giggled. "You could have kissed me in your truck. Remember—the near kiss that turned into the near miss?"

He laughed. "Is that what you call it?"

She gazed at his handsome face. "Why didn't you kiss me, Derek? I think you wanted to."

"I did." His smile faded. "Back then I thought the Lord wanted me to remain single." Looking down, he took her hand in his. "I didn't want to get involved in a relationship, but I know I hurt you." He looked up. "Will you forgive me?"

Cheyenne thought a moment. "Yes, but there's only one way I'll forgive you."

He raised his eyebrows.

"I'll forgive you if we simulate that moment in the truck again." She lifted her tissue to his face. "First I wipe off the mascara. . . ."

He burst out laughing. "This is why I love you so much."

Her eyes widened at him. "Why?"

"You're so much fun." He grinned then cleared his throat.

"Okay, so you're wiping off the mascara."

"Right." She tried not to laugh. "Then I say, 'That's better.'"

"And I say, 'Much better.' And then. . ." His gaze dropped down to her lips, and he leaned in to kiss her.

Cheyenne kissed him back with more passion than before. *I still can't believe this is happening!* But knowing Derek, he would take his time to propose marriage. He might be forty years old before he got around to it.

They were both a little breathless when their kiss ended. Derek sat back and gazed into her eyes. Cheyenne could feel the chemistry between them, and she gave a contented sigh.

Breaking their gaze, Derek looked down. With his free hand, he fumbled in his shirt pocket. "When I was talking to your dad, he gave this to me." Derek pulled out a small velvet box and opened it to reveal two rings, one with a large diamond surrounded by sapphires in a yellow gold setting.

She gasped. "That was my mom's wedding set."

Derek nodded. "Your dad wanted you to have it. He gave it to me when I asked his permission to marry you."

"What?" She looked up at him, and his face blurred as fresh tears clouded her vision. "Are you asking to marry me?"

Raising his eyebrows, he looked a little unsure. "I am. . .if you'll have me."

"Yes I'll have you!" Laughing, she threw her arms around his neck. "Yes, yes!"

He kissed her again. Then he took the rings out of the box. "Let's try these on." Slipping them on her finger, he held up her hand. The rings fit perfectly.

Her eyes widened. "I can't believe they fit."

Derek took her hand and squeezed it. "I think it was meant to be. The Lord made this ring for your finger, just like He made you for me and me for you." He looked at her and winked. "We'll celebrate by going bowling—after I teach you how to ski."

"Derek!" Laughing, she leaned against him.

He kissed her forehead. "Do you realize how God designed

us to complement each other? You're outgoing, and I like to stay in the background. You like adventure, and I like the rut I'm stuck in. But we both want to serve the Lord." He dropped his voice. "And now we can serve Him together."

"Yes." She could barely squeak out the word as tears rushed to her eyes. She cleared her throat. "Do you think we could get married by the end of this year?"

With a shrug, he grinned. "Sure, the sooner the better. But what's the reason?"

She took a deep breath. "I have four million very good reasons. . . ."

epilogue

Two years later

Derek couldn't wipe the smile off his face. He strode through the hospital corridor and passed the nurses' station.

One of the nurses looked up. "Congratulations!"

"Thanks!" His smile grew bigger as he hit the automatic-door button. The two wide doors swung outward. He stepped out and rounded the corner.

The door to the waiting room was closed, and he peered through the small window. His parents sat in the sturdy padded chairs. Dad looked down at an open Bible on his lap. Evidently he was having his morning devotions, and no wonder. It was only seven thirty. Mom sat next to him, knitting something small with yellow yarn.

I know who that's for. The thought made him grin.

Across the room, Cheyenne's dad read a newspaper. His wife, Janet, sat beside him, reading a children's book to Derek's seven-year-old son. Arthur had slimmed down quite a bit since Derek and Cheyenne had adopted him, and he'd grown four inches.

Derek opened the door, and Arthur jumped to his feet. "Hey, Dad! Did Mom have the baby?"

"Yep!" He paused, looking at the five pairs of wide eyes that stared at him. "It's a girl!"

His announcement was met with an outburst of exclamations. Everyone rushed forward and surrounded him. Dad pumped his hand, and Jim slapped him on the back while Mom and Janet both tried to hug him at the same time.

Arthur hopped up and down beside him. "I bet she looks like me, huh, Dad?"

"Not exactly." With a laugh, he motioned for them to follow him. "Cheyenne is waiting for all of you to come visit her—and our daughter."

Mom turned to Janet as they walked out of the room. "We finally got a granddaughter—not that I don't love our little grandsons, mind you."

Janet smiled. "She'll be fun to shop for. I just love looking at little girl dresses."

Derek entered Room 333. He stopped short to gaze at his wife and daughter while his son, his parents, and his parents-in-law surrounded the bed.

Cheyenne sat up with the baby in her arms and gave him a tired smile. Then she took turns hugging everyone. The room echoed with talking and laughter.

"Look at all that dark hair!"

"Her fingers are so little!"

"We'll have to buy some girl's clothes right away."

Mom picked up the baby and cuddled her. "What's her name, Cheyenne? I remember that you and Derek were waffling back and forth on names."

Cheyenne tucked a strand of light-blond hair behind her ear. She glanced up at Derek and smiled before she answered. "We've decided on Arianna."

Janet smiled. "Ooh—that's pretty."

Derek stepped behind Arthur and placed his hands on his son's shoulders. "Since we have one A name, we decided to go for two."

Arthur looked up at him. "Really, Dad? You named her Arianna because of me?"

"Yep. And Arianna's middle name is Lynn, after Cheyenne's mom."

"That's so nice." Janet looked up at Jim as she looped her arm through his, and they shared a smile.

"That reminds me." Derek placed his hand on Cheyenne's shoulder. "The Lynn Wilkins Memorial Wing of the Bolton Creek Children's Home is scheduled to open next week.

You're all invited to the grand opening."

Jim raised his eyebrows. "You've done a lot of good with that money, Derek. I'm proud of you two."

"Knock, knock."

Everyone turned to the door at Callie's voice. She and Lane walked into the room with Lane carrying their little son, Cody, in his arms.

After initial greetings by everyone, Callie walked up to Mom and gazed at the baby. "Oh, she's so pretty."

Cheyenne grinned. "She looks like Derek, so of course she's pretty."

He shrugged. "She got my black hair, Cheyenne. Who knows who she'll look like."

"Yeah, Mom." Arthur leaned against the bed. "I look like you, so Arianna has to look like Dad."

Everyone laughed.

Lane turned to Derek. "Just wait until she's the same age as Cody." He looked down at his son. "This boy gets into everything."

Callie nodded. "And he'll be two years old in six months. The terrible twos. I'm dreading that."

Still holding Arianna, Mom smiled. "Enjoy him while he's little, Callie. Children grow up way too fast." She glanced around the room. "I can't believe we have six grandchildren already."

"And I'm the oldest." Arthur smiled up at her. "Right, Grandma?"

"That's right, Arthur. You'll probably be our first grand-child to get married and start the next generation."

Cheyenne laughed. "Now that's too fast, Mom. I haven't even thought that far ahead."

"That's right. Hold your horses." Derek grinned. "Arthur's only starting second grade this year."

An hour later, the family said their good-byes, and Derek's parents took Arthur with them. He would stay with them in their RV for the next week. But Derek and Cheyenne kept getting visitors, mainly friends from church. The small hospital room began to fill up with flower arrangements, teddy bears, and gift bags of little clothes.

After supper, Tonya and Murray came by. Tonya was still working at The Beauty Spot, but she wouldn't be for long. In two months she would have her own bundle of joy.

Tonya gazed at Arianna. "She is so pretty!"

Murray nodded. "Yep. She looks like a Brandt with the black hair."

"Do you want to hold her, Tonya?" Cheyenne motioned to the chair by the bed. "You can sit there."

"Sure." Tonya took little Arianna in her arms and sat down, her giant belly pushing out her maternity shirt. "You know, I don't think I'm the right shape to hold a baby." She laughed. "I can't wait until ours is born."

"Me, too." Murray turned to Derek and rolled his eyes. "She makes me rub her feet every night."

"Well, they hurt!" Tonya shared a smile with him then cooed to the baby.

Cheyenne lay back against her pillow. "The last month is the worst, Tonya. You'll be ready to have that little one."

"How are your cookbook sales going, sis?" Derek asked.

"Great! Since Lane mentioned it in his newspaper column, sales have boomed."

Murray grinned. "We have so many famous authors in our family."

"We have one." Tonya laughed. "Lane is the only famous person I know."

"You might become another Rachael Ray, Tonya." Cheyenne gave her a tired smile.

❧

After Tonya and Murray left, they had a few more church people come by. Cheyenne was thankful when everyone was gone. She wanted to spend time with her husband and little daughter.

Derek set Arianna in the bassinette by the side of the bed.

Then he pulled Cheyenne into his arms and kissed her. "You are really tired, baby. You need some sleep."

"I know." She gazed into his eyes. "But I've enjoyed this day. Isn't God good to us?"

"He sure is. Let's thank Him." Derek took her hand in his. "Father, thank You for the many blessings You've given us. We especially praise You for our daughter's safe arrival into this world. Please save her at a young age. May she grow up to know You and serve You with her whole heart."

Cheyenne wiped a tear from her eye. *Lord, thank You for giving me such a wonderful husband.*

She had waited, and God had worked out His plan for both of them.

God's plans were always worth waiting for.

Cheyenne's Ten-Layer Enchiladas

    4 cups cooked chicken or turkey, shredded
    1 (14.5 ounce) can diced tomatoes
    1 (10 ounce) can black beans, rinsed
    1 box Rice-a-Roni Mexican-style rice, cooked
    1 cup nacho cheese (queso)
    3 (10 ounce) cans enchilada sauce
    1 package (24 count) yellow-corn tortillas
    1 (4 ounce) can chopped green chilies
    2 cups cheddar cheese, shredded
    1 carton (8 ounce) sour cream

Mix first five ingredients together. In a 9x13-inch pan, make ten layers:

1. Pour 1 cup enchilada sauce in pan to cover bottom.
2. Put 6 corn tortillas on sauce.
3. Spread half of meat mixture on top.
4. Put on another layer of 6 tortillas.
5. Spread 1 cup enchilada sauce mixed with chopped chilies.
6. Put on another layer of 6 tortillas.
7. Spread second half of meat mixture on top.
8. Cover with another layer of 6 tortillas.
9. Pour 1 cup enchilada sauce over all.
10. Top with both cups of shredded cheddar cheese.

Cover with aluminum foil, and bake at 350 degrees for 45 minutes. Uncover and bake for 5 more minutes or until cheese is melted. Serve with sour cream and tortilla chips.

A Letter To Our Readers

Dear Reader:
In order that we might better contribute to your reading enjoyment, we would appreciate your taking a few minutes to respond to the following questions. We welcome your comments and read each form and letter we receive. When completed, please return to the following:

Fiction Editor
Heartsong Presents
PO Box 719
Uhrichsville, Ohio 44683

1. Did you enjoy reading *No One But You* by Donna Reimel Robinson?
   ❏ Very much! I would like to see more books by this author!
   ❏ Moderately. I would have enjoyed it more if

   _____

   _____

   _____

2. Are you a member of **Heartsong Presents**? ❏ Yes ❏ No
   If no, where did you purchase this book? _____

   _____

3. How would you rate, on a scale from 1 (poor) to 5 (superior), the cover design? _____

4. On a scale from 1 (poor) to 10 (superior), please rate the following elements.

   ____ Heroine   ____ Plot
   ____ Hero   ____ Inspirational theme
   ____ Setting   ____ Secondary characters

5. These characters were special because? _____
_____
_____

6. How has this book inspired your life? _____
_____
_____

7. What settings would you like to see covered in future
   Heartsong Presents books? _____
_____
_____

8. What are some inspirational themes you would like to see
   treated in future books? _____
_____
_____

9. Would you be interested in reading other **Heartsong
   Presents** titles? ❏ Yes ❏ No

10. Please check your age range:
    ❏ Under 18   ❏ 18-24
    ❏ 25-34   ❏ 35-45
    ❏ 46-55   ❏ Over 55

Name_____
Occupation _____
Address _____
City, State, Zip_____
E-mail _____

WYOMING WEDDINGS

3 stories in 1

Challenges abound for a truck driving woman, a vacationing police dispatcher, and a guest ranch owner when they encounter threats coinciding with new romances.

Contemporary, paperback, 352 pages, 5.1875" x 8"

── Presents ──

Great Inspirational Romance
at a Great Price!

Heartsong Presents books are inspirational romances in contemporary and historical settings, designed to give you an enjoyable, spirit-lifting reading experience. You can choose wonderfully written titles from some of today's best authors like Wanda E. Brunstetter, Mary Connealy, Susan Page Davis, Cathy Marie Hake, Joyce Livingston, and many others.

When ordering quantities less than six, above titles are $3.99 each.
Not all titles may be available at time of order.